TITAN
BASE

TITAN BASE

• • •

ERIC NYLUND

RANDOM HOUSE 🏠 NEW YORK

Visit us on the Web! randomhouse.com/kids

Educators and librarians, for a variety of teaching tools, visit us at
RHTeachersLibrarians.com

Library of Congress Cataloging-in-Publication Data
Nylund, Eric S.
Titan Base / Eric Nylund. — 1st ed.
p. cm. — (The resisters ; 3)
Summary: Twelve-year-old Ethan must take command of a fractious flying squadron charged with finding a new Resister base, while being pursued by alien invaders.
ISBN 978-0-307-97854-7 (pbk.) — ISBN 978-0-375-97127-3 (lib. bdg.) —
ISBN 978-0-375-98120-3 (ebook)
[1. Science fiction. 2. Extraterrestrial beings—Fiction. 3. Leadership—Fiction.] I. Title.
PZ7.N9948Ti 2013 [Fic]—dc23 2012008449

Printed in the United States of America
10 9 8 7 6 5 4 3 2 1

First Edition

° ° ° CONTENTS ° ° °

TITAN BASE

WEIGHT OF COMMAND

TWELVE-YEAR-OLD ETHAN BLACKWOOD WAITED outside Colonel Winter's office. He fidgeted, because a guard stood at attention at her door. He was an adult master sergeant and he eyed Ethan suspiciously, but the man couldn't ask questions or even tell Ethan to stop staring back.

Ethan was an officer. Sure, the lowest-ranking officer in the entire Resistance, second lieutenant, but still, by the rules, this man's superior.

It made Ethan feel uneasy. What right did he have to outrank an adult Resister who'd been fighting the enemy all his life?

It didn't make any sense.

Colonel Winter called from inside her office: "Enter."

The master sergeant nodded at Ethan and opened the door for him.

Ethan entered and the door shut behind him.

Colonel Winter sat at her huge mahogany desk. She didn't look up at Ethan; rather, she continued to pore over papers on her desk.

Ethan noted that the snow globe of Mount Fuji was no longer on her desk. It had been moved to the bookshelf, next to photos of her son, Sergeant Felix Winter, Ethan's best friend.

How was friendship supposed to work when you were your friend's commanding officer—and his mom was yours?

"At ease, Lieutenant," the colonel said, and finally looked up.

Colonel Winter was the leader of the Resistance. Her dark hair was streaked white down the center. She was cold and hard, and she always looked like she wanted to court-martial someone (usually Ethan).

"You've read your orders?" she asked.

"Yes, ma'am."

Ethan's squadron was supposed to find a suitable location for a new base, in case the Ch'zar found the Seed Bank one day.

Actually, Ethan wondered why this hadn't been done twenty years ago, but he kept his mouth shut. He had learned that was the best thing he could do around Colonel Winter.

"Any questions about the mission?" she asked.

"No, ma'am. I understand the parameters and the consequence of failing," he said. "No questions . . . about the mission."

"About something else, then?" she asked, her eyes narrowing with disapproval. "Don't hedge your words, Lieutenant. I expect all my officers to be candid with their concerns. Consider that a standing order."

Ethan shifted from foot to foot, trying not to squirm like a little kid.

He took a deep breath. "Just one question: Why was *I* put in charge?" He opened his mouth but couldn't seem to get the rest of the words out.

Colonel Winter's frown deepened. "You have permission to speak freely, Lieutenant. Please go on."

"Well, Colonel, no one *asked* me if I wanted to be a second lieutenant. I don't think I'm cut out for command. I want to fight—don't get me wrong—but I'm not sure I should be in charge."

The disapproval on her face vanished. "*That* attitude," she said, "is exactly why I put you in command, Lieutenant."

Ethan shook his head, not getting what she meant.

"When you understand that," she said, "you'll understand what it means to be in charge." She nodded toward the door. "Now, if there's nothing else, I have plans to make. Good flying, Lieutenant. You are dismissed."

Ethan snapped off a crisp salute, turned on his heels, and left her office.

Once outside, he strode directly down the damp concrete corridor to the elevator without looking back. He didn't want the master sergeant at the door to see he'd broken into a cold sweat.

The elevator pinged and the doors opened.

Dr. Irving stood inside.

He was the chief scientist for the Resistance. He wore a white lab coat and had bushy white eyebrows that made him look half surprised all the time, like he was on the verge of a great scientific breakthrough. He was the only adult on base who'd always been nice to Ethan.

"Good morning," Dr. Irving said, and smiled. "Had a pleasant meeting with our colonel, I trust?" His smile turned mischievous, and he added, "No, don't answer that—my idea of a bad joke. Junior officers never have pleasant meetings with the colonel."

Ethan got onto the elevator as the doctor stepped off.

"Dr. Irving?"

The doctor set his hand on the door to stop it from closing. "Yes, young man?"

"What do you think makes someone a good leader?"

Dr. Irving's grin faded. "What makes a good leader? Asking questions like that." He patted Ethan on the shoulder. "I'm sure you'll do fine. In fact, we're all counting on it."

Dr. Irving turned and started down the hallway.

The elevator doors closed, and Ethan was left alone with his thoughts.

He was sure Dr. Irving meant those words as comfort . . . but they had just the opposite effect.

Ethan tugged at his uniform's collar, trying to loosen the single silver lieutenant's bar imprinted there.

It felt like Dr. Irving and Colonel Winter had somehow made the tiny insignia of command weigh fifty pounds.

o o o

classified PRIVATE and CONFIDENTIAL
Pre-mission Log B-728
submitted by Lieutenant Blackwood, Ethan G.
in command of Sterling squadron

BACKGROUND: My pilots are on edge. A month ago, half of them were imprisoned in the Sterling Reform School and thought the world was a safe place, a place full

of rules for them to break and, well, not this world—
swarming with aliens that conquered Earth, giant insect
combat suits, and mind-controlled parents. There's friction between the Sterling recruits (especially Angel) and
the native Resisters. I need to somehow make them work
together.

For the "older" Resisters (Madison, Felix, and Paul),
the stakes are even higher because the Ch'zar came close
to finding our base—aka the Seed Bank. If they *do* find
it, we'll have a fight on our hands we won't be able to win.

I have to keep my cool (or at least look that way for
the rest of the squadron). Is that what a leader is supposed
to do? I'm not sure.

Giving orders is different from getting them. I can cal-
culate the right velocity to make a pinpoint landing or
determine which formation will maximize damage to an
enemy line. But how do I figure out all these "people"
problems?

MISSION OBJECTIVE: Find a new site for a Resister
base. It has to be a place where the Ch'zar would never
look. We're about to go on our seventh scouting sortie,
following Dr. Irving's leads, this one in the ruins of a city
called New Taos.

NOTES: No luck on previous scouting missions. No enemy contact either, thank goodness. After the pasting we gave the Ch'zar in our last battle, I think we won't see them for a long time. The biggest danger in this mission might be boredom.

○ ○ ○ **1** ○ ○ ○

NOT MODEL ROCKETS

ETHAN BRACED HIMSELF. HE COULDN'T STOP shaking from the adrenaline thundering through his body.

He was pretty sure he was about to die.

Surrounded by a faster, deadlier enemy and outnumbered—it qualified for "sitting duck" status.

"*More* incoming missiles!" Madison screamed over the radio. "I now count forty."

These weren't like any Ch'zar missiles Ethan had ever seen. There were no organic parts. In fact, they reminded Ethan of the model rockets he and his sister used to launch. They had rivets and gleaming aluminum hulls, even serial numbers painted on their sides. The one major difference? *These* rockets were thirty feet long and exploded on contact.

Ethan felt smothered inside his cockpit—a closet-like space with blinking indicators, "breathing" air vents, radar screens, and camera displays that tracked missile vapor trails screwing through the air toward his position.

He piloted one of the most advanced fighting craft ever devised: a three-ton mechanical insect hybrid called an insectoid combat exoskeleton (I.C.E. for short). Its armor shrugged off bullets, fire, and crash landings. Its stinger laser could fry through a foot of titanium alloy steel.

If that weren't enough, flying in a wedge formation off his wingtips were the other eight I.C.E.s that made up Sterling Squadron. Together they'd fought off armies and aerial attack groups.

But nothing like this.

These missiles had appeared out of *nowhere*—all closing in on his team at supersonic speeds.

From his vantage point of thirty thousand feet, the attack pattern looked like a gigantic flower blossoming among the fluffy clouds. It was easy to forget it was actually several tons of high-explosive ordnance moving at Mach speeds.

A few missiles . . . he could've dodged, or even survived a direct hit.

But they could never outmaneuver so many. And he couldn't outrun a missile. Even if he could, there was nowhere *to* run. The missiles had them surrounded in a rapidly shrinking circle.

It was a perfect trap.

What really bugged Ethan, though, was that there were no alien Ch'zar units in radar range that could have aimed and fired the stupid things.

Of course, there shouldn't be any Ch'zar out here. This was the middle of a restricted radiation zone, what used to be the southwestern region of the United States. The aliens didn't come out here, because they were smart. That radiation killed you quick.

"Ethan," Felix whispered over a private radio channel. "What do we do?"

Ethan snapped out of it. His thoughts had spiraled out of control.

"Get your head in the game, Blackwood," he told himself.

"Didn't catch that last," Felix said. "Repeat, Lieutenant?"

"Never mind," Ethan growled, angry about freezing up.

He felt the brain of his wasp I.C.E. through a telepathic link. The insect wanted to fly and fight and engage the enemy.

Not this time. That'd just get them all blown up.

Ethan took stock of the battlefield.

The opposing side had forty missiles. They outnumbered Ethan and his team. They had superior acceleration.

On his side were nine I.C.E. units with an arsenal of lasers, bombs, particle cannons, and strength enough to tear through steel like it was tissue paper.

What else? Lots of airspace to fly . . . but in a quickly shrinking circle of death.

Thirty thousand feet below were red rock and sand.

Ethan examined the map on his display. There were latitude and longitude numbers, ground elevation lines, clouds with arrows indicating wind direction, blinking radar contacts, and patterns of undulating green—cool mint that intensified in spots to that fluorescent "puke" green you found on poison warning labels.

That meant radiation.

The fainter green parts were trails of airborne radioactive dust. The bright spots were sources. Superdeadly.

"I got it," Ethan told Felix.

Ethan opened a radio channel with his squadron. "Heat your jets and prime afterburners. Ready on my mark. Follow me in and keep tight."

Sterling Squadron's I.C.E.s hovered close to Ethan's wasp—Felix's gigantic blue rhinoceros beetle, Lee's blur of a housefly, Madison's glittering emerald dragonfly,

Ethan's sister Emma's lethal ladybug, Angel's black wasp, Paul's praying mantis, Oliver's mirror-silver cockroach, and Kristov's blood-red locust.

Armored chitin shifted and jet engines fired with extra power in the collective continuous rumble of a hurricane.

The intense noise reassured Ethan.

They had power. They had speed.

But he'd better be right about this, or they would all be dead, too.

Angel's Nightmare-class black wasp veered close to Madison's dragonfly. The move was aggressive—it looked like Angel was going to pounce on Madison! There'd been some serious hate between those two ever since they'd laid eyes on each other at Sterling. Ethan had no clue why.

At the last second, the black wasp reversed its wings. There was some buffeting back and forth between the two I.C.E.s, and then the wasp swatted at the dragonfly. The dragonfly darted away.

"Hey!" Ethan yelled over the radio. "The enemy is out *there*, you two. Cool it. That's an order!"

Of all the wrong times to fight each other.

Since the Sterling Reform School kids had been added to the group, friction between them and the "old" Resisters had been running hotter than a solar flare.

Madison's and Angel's I.C.E.s settled into formation.

Ethan hissed out his frustration and turned back to the maps on his side displays, tabbing through elevations, trying to get a sense of how the clouds and radioactivity drifted in all three dimensions. He calibrated the screens to wide-view mode—ten miles across so the missiles made a ring around the screens' edges.

The radiation rose ten thousand feet into the air, then bent, wavered, and dissipated in the prevailing winds. It reminded him of movies he'd seen of kelp forests in the ocean. He saw a pattern to it . . . as long as the winds didn't shift.

The missiles were only a few miles away now.

Ethan's heart raced.

His mind slowed.

He took a deep breath.

"Prime for maximum thruster burn," he whispered to his squad. "Ready . . . set . . . go!"

Ethan commanded his wasp to plunge, kicking on jets and afterburners. They plummeted straight toward the ground, breaking the sound barrier with a titanic air-shredding blast.

He tore his gaze from the central display (mesmerized by the ground rushing to meet him) and glanced at his rear-facing camera.

Sterling Squadron was behind him. The other eight

I.C.E.s—all in a tight line with no more than five feet between each.

And behind them, all forty missiles corkscrewed into a hairpin turn and dove, right on their tails.

Just as Ethan had hoped.

His gaze darted to the map of the air currents and radiation.

At three thousand feet he pulled up and rolled over and around a massive radiation plume—but he'd cut it too close!

Alarms sounded inside the cockpit that jangled Ethan's already frayed nerves. The radiation counter strapped to his wrist clicked and whined.

Dr. Irving had warned them about the radiation out here. It was a variety that could be carried by dust.

To protect them, Resistance technicians had sprayed their I.C.E.s with a dust-repellent plastic that would last for a few days. The pilots, meanwhile, had new flight suits and had been given supplements to temporarily boost their radiation tolerance.

Dr. Irving had also given them wristwatch/radiation counters and warned them: *"Once the counter gets to the red line dosage, there's nothing that can be done for you."*

Meaning: Hit the red line on that counter and you're dead.

The needle on Ethan's radiation counter trembled at 15 percent of maximum exposure.

Ethan's hands went sweaty. He tightened his grip on the controls and the wasp rocketed up and out of danger.

The clicking eased and stopped.

Ethan tingled, his face went numb, and his vision fuzzed.

Too much acceleration. Even with the cushioning gel in the cockpit, he couldn't take much more of this.

He glanced back.

His squadron was still behind him.

So were the missiles, closer now, all funneled into a wedge—a gigantic arrowhead of gleaming steel, belching smoke and thunder.

The winds shifted and a huge upwelling of radiation blossomed on-screen.

Ethan dove, almost scraping the ground (and splat-tered a few saguaro cactuses that happened to get in the way into mush).

His vision pinpointed as he and the wasp dodged around the radioactive dust, rock outcroppings, and sand dunes.

The missiles tracked the squadron, closing on a course that was the shortest distance between two points—in this case, cutting *through* airspace filled with radiation.

In pilot training, Ethan had been given quick courses on physics, mostly aerodynamics, but also biology and electronics, and in particular how radiation messed up electronics like tracking and sensor systems.

The lead missile wobbled.

One prematurely detonated.

A third crashed into the missile behind it.

Dozens more piled into them, tumbling along the ground end over end, forty supercharged firecrackers exploding with flashes and glittering shrapnel.

Ethan would have whooped with joy if he hadn't been ready to pass out from spent adrenaline and the punishment of high-g acceleration.

He eased back his throttle and exhaled.

The wasp settled in the shade of a small mesa without being commanded to do so.

Sterling Squadron followed him.

Ethan let his wasp ground. He sensed it was uncharacteristically tired, too. Maybe the radiation?

He glanced at his wrist with dismay. The radiation counter marked 20 percent of the way to a maximum dosage. It wouldn't go back down until he got specialized medical attention at the Seed Bank base.

Ethan hit the outer door release. Armored sections

hissed away from the I.C.E.'s abdomen and he practically fell out of the cockpit.

It was broiling hot outside. He felt like passing out. Around him an ocean of sand dunes wavered with mirages.

His wasp scooched farther into the shade.

Lee climbed out of his housefly I.C.E., his normally wild black hair sweat-plastered to his head. Kristov clenched and unclenched his huge fists (mostly to keep them from shaking too much). Angel dropped out of her black wasp, looking like she did this every day and it was no big deal. Paul got out of his "Crusher" praying mantis, and his scarred face was grim. Madison exited her dragonfly and shot a glare at Angel that was hotter than any laser beam. Felix and Emma marched side by side straight toward Ethan.

"That was close," Emma said. She took a wisp of black hair that'd escaped her braid and chewed the end. Her nervous habit. It was gross.

"Those missiles didn't look like Ch'zar," Felix said.

He'd shaved stripes into the side of his close-cropped hair before this mission—for luck, he'd said.

"Yeah," Ethan agreed. "I never saw one enemy I.C.E. on-screen."

Madison started toward Angel, her lips pursed, her

hands balled into fists. Madison was a martial arts expert and deadly fast. It looked like she was going to tear Angel in half for that stunt in the air.

As the two of them faced off, they looked like opposites to Ethan: Madison, with her long blond hair, completely serious, and Angel, her short dark hair cut at a weird slant over her eyes, never serious.

Madison abruptly halted in her tracks. She gazed at the sky and slowly turned in a circle.

"We didn't see any Ch'zar in the air shooting missiles," she told Ethan, "because those missiles weren't fired from the air."

She pointed at the dozens of vapor trails in the sky.

Ethan traced the lines back to ground level. "Surface-to-air missiles?" he said. He'd never seen the Ch'zar use them. They favored ant lion artillery. He clambered on top of a rock to get a better look.

Exhaust trails made a fading circle, three miles wide in the sky. The center where the missiles had been launched was only a mile from their current position.

Ethan squinted. Through the mirage-wavering heat, he saw towers and domes, intact and gleaming gold under the desert sun.

It was the city they were looking for. Maybe not as dead and abandoned as they'd thought.

∘ ∘ ∘ 2 ∘ ∘ ∘

A FORCE DIVIDED

ETHAN STARED AT THE DISTANT CITY, HIS MOUTH open.

Ruby-red spires rose a half mile into the sky, so delicate they seemed to float. There were geodesic domes that shimmered golden in the hot air, and inside those domes were trees and waterfalls and even wisps of rainbow-tinged fog. Slender sky bridges arched between the tallest towers, with rows of glimmering green lights on their lengths. Crows circled the place, riding the thermal currents.

It wasn't like the other pre-Ch'zar human city, Knucklebone Canyon, Ethan had seen near Mexico. That place had been toppled over, half concrete rubble, half rusted steel girders—like a bomb had gone off in the middle of it (and considering it'd been destroyed in World War IV, that's probably what *did* happen).

But this place was perfect. Every surface and window was a polished mirror. It looked like the cover of one of the science-fiction comics Ethan used to read at Barker's Drugstore in Santa Blanca.

Felix and Emma got onto the rock next to him.

"Wow," Felix said, squinting and scratching his head.

The other Sterling pilots clambered up as well.

"That can't be," Paul whispered, frowning.

"Why not?" Kristov asked, and turned, almost knocking skinny Paul off the rock, he was so large.

"Because," Madison told him, "that's a *human* city, stupid. One from before the Ch'zar came. It can't be intact . . . or inhabited. The aliens disassembled most human cities for scrap metal and parts."

"Maybe this place is too radioactive," Felix said. He folded his big arms over his chest.

"But if the Ch'zar can't survive here," Oliver whispered, "then that means humans can't either, right?"

They were all quiet a moment.

Emma snorted. "Well, *someone* has to be home," she said. "Someone, or something, fired those missiles at us."

That last comment snapped Ethan back.

He had a mission to carry out: find a new base for the Resisters.

Maybe this city was it. Emma was right, though. Someone—Ch'zar or human—*had* fired missiles at them from the place. That meant a potential enemy.

"It has to be the radiation," he told his team. "I mean, why the city is still in one piece. This desert has so many hot spots and radioactive dust plumes, no one in their right mind would come here."

Angel let her bangs fall over her eyes. "Except us," she murmured.

Ethan glanced at the radiation counter on his wrist. Was it his imagination or had it ticked up a notch closer to the red line? No. Still at 20 percent of a lethal dosage. Still, too much.

Ethan hopped off the rock. He returned to the I.C.E.s clustered in the shadow of the small mesa. The insects had the sense to stay out of the direct sun.

His team gathered around him.

Ethan wiped the sweat off his face and looked at his squadron. They were scared. He could practically feel the fear trembling in the air.

Ch'zar they could fight. Dodge missiles even, no prob-lem. But the radiation around them was invisible. Too much exposure and no medicine in the world would save them. None of them knew how to fight *that*.

Except, whatever lived in that city seemed to be okay with the radiation. Unless they were all dead, too . . . like this was a ghost city.

Despite the desert heat, a shudder jangled down Ethan's back.

Everyone in the squadron was looking to him for answers.

He didn't have any, but Ethan knew they were depending on him. And he knew, scared or not, they were ready to follow orders.

That is, everyone except possibly Angel.

She flipped her hair from her face and popped her gum like she didn't care. Maybe she *did* care and her act of "not caring" was her way of dealing with it.

Madison watched Ethan as he looked at Angel, and then Madison's gaze turned to the girl as well, and her eyes narrowed to slits.

That was one more lethal danger out here—those two might kill each other before the Ch'zar could get them.

Ethan had to solve that problem. Fast.

"I'm taking a small team to scout the city," he said.

He nodded to his sister and his best friend and then

pinned the most troublesome of the Sterling school kids with a stare. "Emma, Felix, and Angel, you're with me," he said. "Everyone else stays here."

"What?" Paul cried, and his hands flew up in a gesture of outrage. "There's no way I'm staying here with these guys—babysitting!"

Kristov clenched his jaw and moved toward Paul.

Madison stepped between them. "Cool it, you idiots. The lieutenant's given his orders."

She shot Ethan a venomous look that said, *You better explain fast or there'll be mutiny . . . starting with me.*

"Madison has to stay," Ethan explained, "in case we need to get a message to the Seed Bank. Her dragonfly has the best chance to get past any missiles or the Ch'zar if they show up—and out of the radiation zone that's blocking long-range radio transmissions."

"So why leave the rest of us?" Oliver said, pushing up his glasses, trying and failing to hide his disappointment.

"Worst-case scenario," Ethan told him. "If there's trouble, the rest of you have to help Madison get a message back to base."

Paul counted out four fingers. "Makes sense. But me, Lee, Oliver, and Kristov, that's four. You only need three for a flight team. Why the extra?"

Ethan nodded to the giant insects nestled in the shade. "I'll need one of you to stay and guard our I.C.E.s, because we're going in on foot."

Paul didn't look happy at this, but then a mischievous grin flickered over his face before he could hide it.

"Under no circumstances are you to fly the I.C.E.s toward that city, Paul. That's an order. Got it?"

Paul grimaced, making the scars on his face pucker, but he nodded.

"If we fly in," Ethan went on, "we risk whatever fired those missiles spotting the I.C.E.s and shooting us down."

"So, we're walking in instead and getting blown up without our combat suits?" Angel asked.

"I don't think so," Felix told her. "Birds are flying around the city. No one's shooting *them* down. On foot, we should be small enough to sneak in without getting noticed."

Angel looked the big guy up and down, and then shrugged.

Ethan waited for more questions, but no one said anything. His people might not like his orders, but they believed in him. He wished he had half the confidence in himself that they seemed to have.

He wanted to sit down and rest, because it felt like the heat was hammering on them, even in the shade. Ethan couldn't look weak, though, in front of his squadron. He

fidgeted with the collar of his flight suit. That silver lieutenant's bar seemed to dig into his neck no matter what
he did.

"Okay, grab your gear," he ordered.

Felix, Emma, and Angel marched to their I.C.E.s.

He went to his wasp. The hairs on the gigantic insect's
gold-and-black-striped armor bristled as he neared, sensing his presence. Its never-blinking eyes tracked him as he
approached.

Madison followed Ethan. "You need a hand?"

"Sure."

Ethan took off his flight gloves and pressed his palm to
the external cargo panel. A section of the wasp's exoskeleton hissed and hinged aside. Inside was a small space
with a backpack containing field rations, a medical kit, water, survival gear, a radio (useless except at short range in
this radiation zone), and signal flares.

There was also another small pack that held the precious things he couldn't leave behind, no matter how dangerous this mission might be. First, there were three
chocolate and hazelnut ration bars he'd liberated from the
Seed Bank's mess. They were his favorites (probably a
half-melted mess in this heat, though). Second was the
leather band Madison had given him. It had an electrical
resistor sewn on. It was the symbol every Resister pilot

carried. It had been Madison's brother's . . . before he had his mind taken over by the Ch'zar. It had been a huge gift to give Ethan, and it meant that he had been accepted as one of them. Third, and most precious to him, was the goodbye note his parents had left him back in Santa Blanca. It'd been folded into neat quarters. He'd read it so many times, the corners were worn round.

He'd never see his parents again. The note was his only connection to them.

He grabbed an extra water bottle and drank the whole thing—partly because he was parched, partly because there was a lump of homesickness in his throat.

"Your orders stink," Madison told him with a huff. "Don't worry. I'll follow them, but we'd be better off *without* Angel."

Ethan wasn't sure if he disagreed. But Angel had left Sterling to help them fight the Ch'zar. She was part of the team. Ethan had a responsibility to help her, didn't he?

But what if Angel caused an accident? Got someone killed?

Ethan stared into Madison's green eyes . . . and got a weird feeling this wasn't entirely about Angel.

Madison inched closer, so close he felt her breath on his face. "Just be careful out there, Blackwood. If anything happens to you, well, I mean, I . . . the rest of us, the Resistance needs you."

Ethan felt himself flushing even hotter in the broiling desert heat. Something like adrenaline shot through his blood (but not exactly adrenaline).

It had to be the jitters about this upcoming mission.

"I'm coming back," he whispered to her. "Count on it, Corporal."

Madison leaned even closer, so near that Ethan felt her body heat on his skin—then she whirled around to face Felix, who had walked up behind her.

Felix looked at both of them, suddenly embarrassed. "Oh . . . sorry."

"There's nothing to be sorry about," Madison said, flustered. She punched Felix halfheartedly in the gut. "Just bring these rookies back, okay?"

Felix nodded. "I always have."

Madison cast one more glance back at Ethan, frowned, and jogged to Paul and the others.

Felix raised an eyebrow at Ethan as if to ask what that was all about.

Ethan shrugged in reply. He didn't have a clue.

They walked over to Emma and Angel. The two girls helped each other strap down their packs.

Angel's black wasp watched Ethan and opened and snapped shut its jaws with a *snikt*.

"We're good to go," Emma said.

"Sure, we're great," Angel said. "A march over open ground in broad daylight, in the middle of enemy territory. What's not perfect about that?"

"It's actually smart," Felix told her. "No one detected enemy radar locks in that missile barrage. They must've used thermal imagers to home in on our I.C.E.s' body heat, which runs boiling hot in flight mode, not to mention the heat from our jet engines."

Emma wiped the sweat off her freckled face. "I get it," she said, a slight bit of approval in her tone. "In this desert our thermal signature should blend into the background heat."

Ethan nodded. That wasn't exactly what he had in mind. He just figured if the enemy had more missiles and could detect them, then they would've *already* blasted them into atoms.

Paul, Madison, Kristov, Oliver, and Lee then gathered before them.

"Good luck, Lieutenant," Paul said, and then muttered, "You're going to need it."

Ethan wondered if he and Paul would ever be friends. Probably not. But he knew Paul would do the right thing, because they were on the same side fighting the Ch'zar. Maybe he wasn't a good friend, but Paul was a decent person under all his scars and attitude.

Ethan snapped off a salute, gave Madison a long look (she glanced down, unable to meet his eyes), and then turned, and the scouting party marched into the desert . . . toward that ghost city.

DIFFERENT

I.C.E. FLIGHT SUITS WERE MADE FOR HIGH-G COM-
bat maneuvers, not strolls in the desert at midday. It was
like walking through an oven wearing a plastic bag. The
internal moisture pads were soaked and squished with
each step Ethan took.

Of course, Ethan and his team had to keep the suits on
for the extra radiation protection.

Dr. Irving had also upgraded their flight suits so the
insect chromo skin cells adapted to their surroundings.
Ethan's suit, normally yellow and black to match his wasp,
had transformed into sand brown and red stone patterns.

From a distance he bet he blended perfectly with the desert.

Ethan looked over his shoulder, squinting in the heat.

Marching single file behind him were Emma, Angel, and Felix—all semicamouflaged, all looking as miserable as Ethan.

They trudged along like that for a half hour. Around them were sand dunes, broken rock . . . and Ethan could barely see the mesa wavering in the heat where he'd left the rest of his squadron.

He held up a hand and said, "Break."

They stopped and guzzled water from their bottles.

Ethan had a faint buzzing sensation in his head. *It must be the heat . . . or the radiation.*

He consulted his map for the tenth time in the last few minutes. Ethan traced the dotted line that marked their progress. The map had a compass and sensor that counted their steps and could give their position to five decimal places in terms of latitude and longitude. Their path couldn't be a straight line because they had to dodge radiation hot spots or get cooked.

So far he'd done an okay job. The counter on his wrist hadn't ticked up once toward the lethal red line.

He swallowed. Despite the quart of water he'd just

chugged, his mouth still felt like sandpaper. This was like walking through a minefield.

Ahead on the map were more hot spots. They blocked the Resisters' path with vile green poison splotches. They'd have to go west to avoid one, and that'd lead them to a strange red-black patch on the map. Ethan couldn't zoom in on that area and tell what it was, because their map no longer received data from the satellite network overhead.

"Come on," he told his team, "we've got to keep moving."

"How about a rest, Captain Gung Ho?" Angel said. She bent over and rested her hands on her knees. Her sweat-soaked black bangs were plastered to her forehead.

"Yeah," Emma said, and closed her eyes. "Just five minutes. We're going to get heatstroke in these suits."

"We can't," Ethan told them. "Our map isn't getting any updates, so I can't read the wind patterns. One stray gust could blow radioactive dust right into our faces."

Angel grimaced, stood, and staggered, but shook her head to clear it. "Right," she whispered. "Move and get heatstroke . . . or stand still and get cooked by radiation."

Felix moved closer to her, ready to catch her if she fainted.

She didn't, though, and marched ahead of Ethan. She was stronger than she looked.

Ethan folded his map and caught up to her. He would have felt sorry for Angel if she wasn't always saying stupid things like that. He needed to tell her to keep her demoralizing opinions to herself. Before he could say anything, though, she spoke.

"I don't get you, Blackwood." She looked him over, disapproval etched across her face. "You don't fit."

Ethan tugged at the collar of his flight suit. "What are you talking about?"

She lowered her voice to a whisper. "You stuck out at Sterling. It was so obvious you weren't one of *us*."

Angel glanced back at Felix. "But you're not one of *them* either. Those Seed Bank guys—all duty, all the time. You do a fair imitation, but I can tell that you and your sister are . . . different. You're different from *everyone*. There's more to it than just coming from a neighborhood, isn't there?"

He was about to tell her to save her breath for the hike, but she was right.

Ethan wasn't a delinquent like the other Sterling kids. A lifetime of living in rule-bound Santa Blanca has guaranteed that.

But he *did* break rules.

It's how he'd stayed alive. How he'd won against the Ch'zar.

That wasn't the way the Seed Bank Resisters worked. They followed orders.

So what were he and Emma? Why were they here?

His parents had said Ethan and his sister weren't like anyone else. They were smarter. Tougher. And they were able to think for themselves.

"We're just trying to make the best of it," he finally told Angel. "Trying to stay alive and keep our minds."

"Right, Blackwood. Look, why don't you just admit it?" She cast a sly glance his way. "Then you and I can be 'different' from the rest of these losers together." She winked at him.

Ethan didn't answer her. He kept walking.

He couldn't stop thinking, though, about what Angel had said.

One reason he'd joined the Resisters was to find answers to why he was different—and why his parents were different. They'd been adults living inside the Ch'zar Collective and somehow keeping their minds.

If he'd really been true to the Resisters, he would've told Dr. Irving or Felix or Madison about *that*. At first he'd thought the Resisters might study him or suspect he was a spy for the aliens if they knew about his parents. But they wouldn't do those things now, after all he'd done.

So why hold back?

They marched over a sand dune, and just ahead Ethan saw what that red-and-black splotch on the map was: a field of junk.

It was the size of a city block and was filled with old robot suits like the ones Ethan had piloted when playing soccer back at Northside Elementary. There were stacks of refrigerators and piles of tin cans. Some objects he barely recognized, they were so rusty—and they crumbled into dust as he approached.

"Creepy," Emma whispered. She grabbed her braid and fiddled with it.

"At least those athletic suits aren't active," Felix whispered back.

Ethan said nothing, remembering how they'd battled teachers in similar suits at Sterling. He imagined these rusted hulks coming to life, chasing and crushing them.

Angel inhaled and tensed like she was gathering her last bit of energy for a fight.

But the long-dormant suits lay there, inert.

Ethan led them through stacks of spooled copper wire, plastic barrels filled with ball bearings. He skirted a pile of broken glass the size of a house, emerging on the other side of the junkyard.

They faced a thirty-foot wall of smooth stainless steel. This was the edge of New Taos.

From a distance, the place had sparkled like a gem in the desert. Up close, though, streaks of rust painted the metal wall, and up and over that wall, Ethan could see the glass domes had spiderweb cracks and the crystalline spires were covered with bird poop.

The city felt completely empty.

As if she could read his mind, Emma leaned closer and said, "But we saw *something* moving inside those domes. It can't all be empty. We just have to get over that wall. We can't see anything from down here."

Angel moved to the wall, reached out, and then jerked her hand away. "Too hot!" she hissed. "Even with gloves."

Felix smoothed a hand over his shorn head. "It's sunny on this side," he said. "There has to be shade on the other, right?"

Ethan nodded and they stomped around to the opposite side of the city. Any chance of Paul and the others seeing them through binoculars vanished as they rounded the curved wall and went out of sight.

Since their radios didn't work because of the intervening radiation, the only way Ethan could get help was with the signal flares in his pack—which would also alert any potential enemies.

On the plus side, as they crossed into the shade, the desert heat dropped ten degrees.

Angel reached out once more and touched the metal wall. "Still bloody hot," she told him, "but it should be okay for a bit."

She shrugged off her pack and pulled out a rope with a gecko-grip grapple. Without waiting for orders, she tossed it over the edge of the wall. It stuck on the first try.

She started up the rope, but Ethan set his hand over hers. "I'll go," he told her. "Lieutenant's prerogative. You take a breather."

The real reason Ethan wanted to go first was he didn't know what she'd do up there by herself. Something crazy.

Angel jerked her hand from his. She stared at it and then at him. Her heart-shaped face crinkled with anger . . . then confusion . . . and then she took a step back, and Ethan could've sworn she almost looked afraid.

Ethan had never seen Angel look scared.

She acted like no one had ever touched her.

Could that be true? What if the only time Angel had ever let anyone else touch her had been at Sterling—with their fists in those mock combats? She'd said Ethan was "different" and that he "stuck out" . . . but what was *her* story?

"Sorry," he whispered.

Angel nodded, seeming to accept the apology (but she nonetheless rubbed her hand).

Ethan grabbed the rope.

"I'm right up after you," Emma told him in that older-sister, don't-argue-with-me tone.

"Good," he said. "Then Angel. Felix last."

Felix scanned the skies overhead, squinting. "If I spot anything, I'll give the rope two hard tugs."

Without further discussion (although Ethan felt a full swarm of butterflies in his stomach and desperately wanted to procrastinate and talk more), he clambered up.

The residual heat of the metal, even on this shaded side, penetrated his flight boots. The polymer soles got soft and sticky. He couldn't imagine trying to scale the wall in the full sun. He'd have melted to the side!

He grunted as he pulled himself over the top. The wall was six feet thick, so it was easy to lie flat. He wormed his way to the far edge and stared, astonished.

Below in the streets and along the arching bridges there were robots.

Lots of them. Everywhere.

Ethan counted dozens, moving back and forth—some in obvious patrol patterns, others speeding along on their single wheel on some urgent mission. These weren't like the rusted suits in the metal graveyard outside the city. These robots gleamed with polished steel and oiled hydraulics. They were similar to the athletic suits he'd played soccer in but had one wheel instead of legs and slitted helmets for heads. In either hand they held parabolic communication dishes.

There were no human pilots. Where one would have sat inside, there were heavy-duty hydraulic pistons and a bluish glow.

Ethan's skin crawled. He knew what that glow was.

He'd seen it once before when one of his team's athletic suits had gotten straight-armed into a goalpost. There had been a coolant leak in the tiny nuclear reactor, and Coach Norman had explained that the glow emanating from the reactor was a special type of radiation. Hazard teams had come and cleaned it all up, but the field had still been off-limits for an entire semester.

That's all he needed now: *more* radiation.

To top it all off, the buzzing headache he'd felt earlier was back, louder now.

Emma wormed up onto the wall and crawled over him, planting her knee in his back in the process, and then lay flat next to him.

"This is bad," she whispered.

"Shhhhh!" Ethan hissed at her. Was she crazy, making noise up here?

At his shush, though, the nearest robot froze, swiveled, and pointed both its handheld parabolic dishes toward their position on the wall.

Ethan and Emma ducked and froze.

He counted thirty thundering heartbeats and then risked a peek over the edge.

The machine had moved on.

Angel pulled herself up and wedged between him and Emma.

"Wow," she mouthed, at least having the good sense to be quiet.

Felix came up last, and despite his bulk, stayed low.

One of the robots on a nearby bridge squealed to a halt, practically skidding sideways on its one wheel. It brandished its parabolic hand dishes back and forth on the surface ahead.

Ethan squinted.

A single tiny cockroach skittered from one shadow on the bridge—then made a dash for the other side.

A glow sparked within the robot's head and intensified. A particle beam flashed, half lightning, half purple laser beam.

The cockroach flared and popped. The metal bridge where it'd been a second before glowed with an orange heat spot. The robot inspected the smoldering bits and then, satisfied, sped along its way.

Ethan and the others pushed back from the edge.

"Whoa," Emma murmured. "If those things can *hear* a cockroach at ten paces, we'll be fried before we can take three steps down there."

"We need our I.C.E.s," Felix said, and his big hands involuntarily curled into fists as if he was ready to fight all those robots.

Ethan agreed (although how they'd fly their suits past the city's missile-defense system would be the problem).

"Come on," Ethan said. "We're not going to learn anything up here other than how to get fried by robot particle beams." He turned back to the rope but saw Angel crawl on her stomach farther along the wall, craning her head to see something that'd caught her attention.

He followed her. What insane thing was she going to try now?

She held one finger to her lips and pointed to a silver dome a hundred yards away.

Carved into a marble arch over the dome's entrance was a single word: LIBRARY.

° ° ° **4** ° ° °

GOING WITH PLAN B

"SURE, IT'S CRAZY," ETHAN TOLD HIS SISTER. "I'M not denying that."

The four Resisters faced each other, propped up on their elbows. Their flight suits had adapted to the new surroundings by taking on a silver sheen streaked with rust. They nonetheless stayed low on the wall so they wouldn't risk being spotted.

Emma was all scowls and seriousness. Felix looked at him as if Ethan had bonked his head. Angel, though, was bright eyed and smiling (it was the first time he'd noticed how pretty that was, too).

"We're running out of time," Ethan said. "If we go back

for our I.C.E.s and then somehow get back here without alerting those robots or triggering the city's missile-defense system, we just risk *more* radiation exposure."

He glanced at the radiation counter on his wrist. It'd gone up one more tic since they'd cleared the junkyard. That was 21 percent toward the untreatable, lethal limit line.

He gulped.

"So we risk getting killed by robots instead?" Emma asked with maximum sarcasm.

"We won't," Ethan said. "I'll toss my water bottle, and with those supersensitive antennae, the noise will definitely get their attention. Then we slide down the second line."

He shook the second rope he'd attached with the gecko grapple. It lay coiled, ready to be tossed over the other side of the wall into the city.

"It'll be an easy sprint to the library," he said. "If there are any answers about this place or information about other intact cities, they'll be there."

"That's not our mission, though," Felix said with a shake of his head. "We're supposed to see if *this* place could make a new base for the Resistance. With hostiles all over, I think that's a no."

"It's our mission to find a new site for a Resistance base," Ethan said. "Whatever that takes."

It bothered him that his best friend, the person who would follow him almost anywhere, wasn't supporting him when he needed it the most.

"Look," Ethan continued, "what if we figure out a way to turn off the robots? Or reprogram them so they follow our orders? This has to be human technology from before the Ch'zar invasion. We could find a way to use it."

"We better go back." Emma examined the counter on her wrist, frowned, and massaged her forehead like she had a splitting headache, too. "We need to get treated for the radiation we've absorbed so far; then we can return with a better plan."

Ethan ground his teeth, annoyed . . . but then he thought about it.

Emma was no coward.

His sister was smart. Sometimes—he hated to admit it—*smarter* than him.

So why did he still feel like he had to get into that library *right now*? Pushing so hard he might get them all killed?

Maybe because he wanted more than answers about the city's defenses.

Answers like how the humans here had resisted the Ch'zar invasion.

Answers like how an adult person could avoid the alien mind control . . . like Ethan's parents.

But no answers were worth getting melted by a plasma beam for.

"Okay . . . ," Ethan admitted. "You two are right, so—"

He noticed that Angel had belly-crawled away from them.

She jumped to her feet.

"I'm up here!" she shouted, and waved at every robot in the city. She grabbed the first rope, making a big show of starting to rappel down the outer wall. "Catch me if you can, you mechanized unicycles!"

Ethan felt his stomach drop into his boots.

Every robot in sight, dozens and dozens of them, halted on ramps, on bridges, and in doorways. Their antennae swiveled toward Angel. Each of them turned and sped to a gate in the wall.

Ethan grabbed for Angel's leg.

She was too quick, though, and slid down the rope.

She called up, "Don't worry—I'll lose them in the junkyard. Double back. You'll only have a minute. So make it count!"

Angel popped her gum and was gone down the rope.

Ethan peered over the edge. He couldn't believe her!

This was beyond crazy. Sure, *he'd* done something just like it back at Ward Zero in Sterling, but that was different. Part of a plan.

This was totally insane.

Angel ran flat out to the junkyard.

Robots emerged from the city's gate, chasing her and fanning out, leaving clouds of dust in their wake.

"She's psychotic," Emma whispered.

Ethan agreed, but he also couldn't help but admire a tiny bit such raw fearlessness.

"We sure can't go back that way," Felix said. He tossed down their second rope on the city side. "Guess we're going with Plan B."

Ethan wavered. He wanted to run after Angel and save her from herself. She was part of his squadron, and he was responsible for her.

But there was no way he could chase after her with those robots between them. They'd hear Ethan and get them *all*.

On the other hand, she *had* maneuvered to give Ethan a shot at getting to that library. If by some miracle Angel survived and doubled back, they'd better be there waiting for her, or they might not ever find her again.

Ethan grabbed the rope, slid down, and landed hard inside the city.

Emma followed, almost on top of him. Felix then thudded to the ground.

No robots.

Ethan sprinted. He felt like a bad leader for leaving one of his team behind. Maybe that's what leaders were supposed to do. He wasn't sure.

The streets were paved with interlocking blocks of steel and green-tinged copper. Many buildings were made of glass. A few looked like they had been grown from crystals.

It was beautiful. And empty.

Seeing it all deserted sent a shiver down his spine.

Ethan ran straight for the geodesic dome of the library—through its white marble entrance arch and into the darkness beyond.

⚬ ⚬ ⚬ 5 ⚬ ⚬ ⚬

WAY OVERDUE AT THE LIBRARY

ETHAN SKIDDED TO A HALT AND HIS EYES AD-justed to the darkness.

A dim light came from ahead.

He eased forward and peered down a huge spiral in the floor, at least a full soccer field across, that wormed into the earth as far as he could see.

The light came from the curved walls of this gigantic spiral. Along them, segmented panels of illumination softly flickered.

He turned, and as his eyes continued to adjust, he saw the same walls on this ground level. Each wall had shelves filled with blocks of crystal. Some of the crystals were amethyst purple, others a golden topaz, still others ruby red, but most were clear and glimmered like diamonds. He squinted and saw that inside each block was the twinkle of diodes and other delicate circuitry.

It had to be a computer. Or since this was a library . . . electronic books? But not any type of book he'd ever seen before.

"This place is too weird," Emma whispered, and rubbed her temples. "It feels . . . hollow."

Hollow was right. Ethan felt as if his head were hollow, made of metal and buzzing even louder now than it had been before with a strange, almost musical rhythm.

That had to be his imagination.

"I don't like it either," Felix murmured. "Too quiet."

Felix stepped closer to Emma, and Ethan wasn't sure because of the murky light, but he could've sworn he grabbed her hand.

The lights flickered on—coming from the walls, the ceiling, and even the floor.

Ethan blinked in the sudden brightness.

"Is there anything I can help you with?" a mechanized voice asked.

Ethan yelped and spun around. He faced one of the city's robots.

It was close enough to touch—and close enough to clobber him flat.

It'd been hard to judge the size of these things up on the wall, but this near, it towered ten feet over him and must've weighed twice as much as a normal athletic suit since there was a giant nuclear reactor where the cockpit should've been.

The robot balanced on one wheel, swaying back and forth. It looked down on him and the others, but not with the same slitted helmet as the guard robots. This robot had a blank face that glowed with a soft white spot. Instead of ultrasensitive antennae in its hands, this one's hands were normal (if "normal" was six fingers on a white-gloved hand big enough to hold three basketballs at once).

"Wh-what did you say?" Ethan sputtered. He was terrified. It was the best he could do.

"I am the librarian," it told them. "I asked, young citizen, if there is anything I can help you with."

Ethan almost fell over backward.

A lucky break. Finally.

"We're looking for answers," Ethan said.

The robot librarian spread its arms wide in a friendly gesture. "I am here to serve."

"Perfect," Emma whispered to Ethan. She gave him a rare nod of approval.

Ethan noted that she and Felix no longer held hands. They weren't even standing next to each other . . . pretending that never happened.

He was about to tell them that everything was going to be okay now—that they'd figure out how to turn off those guardian robots, that they'd be the heroes of the Resistance—when he heard clicking from his wrist.

Ethan's radiation counter ticked up as he watched.

He instinctively took two steps back from the librarian.

Emma's counter clicked away, too. Her eyes locked onto the nuclear reactor glowing ghostly blue in the robot's chest.

"What questions do you have?" the librarian asked, wheeling closer.

Felix stepped between them to stop it from getting nearer to Emma. His counter clicked away even faster.

"Where is everyone?" Felix demanded. "I mean, the people of New Taos?"

Emma pulled Felix back—and this time held on to the big guy's hand.

"Ah . . ." The librarian paused. One hand contemplatively tapped its featureless face. "File synopsis retrieved. New Taos is currently experiencing a stage IV evacuation due to elevated radiation levels. All citizens must report to a transportation station after their duty shift. This situation will be momentarily corrected."

"Just how long is 'momentarily'?" Ethan asked.

The librarian hesitated even longer before answering. "Restoration efforts are delayed by mandatory system repairs due to elevated radiation levels," it told Ethan. "Current project estimate is . . . one hundred thirty-eight years."

Ethan's hopes of using this place for a Resistance base evaporated. One hundred thirty-eight years? That might as well be forever.

"That's why there's a junkyard out there," Felix whispered. "Even mechanical men can't last long here."

"There's *no way* we can use anything here," Emma whispered back, and her forehead crinkled with frustration. "Ethan, let's get the heck out of here!"

Ethan held up his hands to calm his sister. "Just a few more questions."

They'd come this far. They were still within safe radiation exposure levels (although that could change *fast* if he wasn't careful). And this librarian had so much information that could prove useful to the Resistance . . . and to Ethan.

Emma released Felix's hand and crossed her arms over her chest. "It doesn't matter what I say, does it? You're going to stay anyway."

Ethan pursed his lips and said nothing.

She sighed and glared at her radiation counter. "When this gets to thirty percent, I'm going to mutiny, Lieutenant, knock you over the head, and drag you out of here!"

Felix gave Ethan a little nod.

Ethan wasn't sure if that meant he agreed with him that they should get more data or he agreed with Emma about carrying him out of here against his will.

Ethan turned back to the librarian.

The nuclear reactor in the robot's chest seemed to glow even brighter.

Ethan had to be crazy for staying here. He didn't care, though. He *needed* answers. He wasn't sure *why* he needed them so badly . . . it was like that hollow metal sensation in his head was something in his brain waiting to be filled.

He'd start with the most practical questions.

"Can the guardian robots be ordered to stand down? Or the city's missile-defense system turned off?"

"Yes, young citizen. However, level III authorization codes are required."

Ethan didn't have a clue what those were, but he *was* sure he didn't have them. That eliminated the possibility of getting their I.C.E.s for a quick evacuation.

"So the Ch'zar were never in this city?"

"I have no record of the word *Ch'zar* in my database," the librarian replied.

Ethan finally gave in to his feelings and asked what he *really* wanted to know instead of skirting the issue.

"So no records of mind control either?"

The librarian froze for a few seconds. Its reactor pulsed. "Mind control?" it replied. "No. But there are records on mind *expansion*—extrasensory perception—group-thought protocols, and, of course, Project Prometheus."

Prometheus.

The word filled the void in Ethan's mind like a perfect jigsaw-puzzle piece.

He remembered it from history class—mentioned by his teacher in passing during the mythology unit. When Ethan's parents saw the name on his homework, though, they made a *huge* deal about it. They checked out books from the Santa Blanca library and made Ethan read everything there was about Prometheus.

According to legend, Prometheus stole fire from the gods and gave it to humankind. The ancient Greeks believed people would still be cavemen without Prometheus.

Ethan's parents had often said he was like Prometheus—clever, doing whatever it took to win—and when he got in trouble (like after he shot his model rockets into the neighbor's garage), they had reminded him that Prometheus had also been *punished* by the gods, chained to a rock while his liver was torn out by a giant eagle.

Supergross.

His skin pebbled with chill bumps.

"Tell me everything about Prometheus," Ethan demanded. "No, wait—can I check out a book on that subject?"

He was an idiot. This was, after all, a library. He should check out the data he wanted instead of talking with a machine while he was not so slowly fried by radioactivity.

The librarian snapped its fingers.

A smaller version of the librarian appeared from the shadows. It raced to a nearby shelf, ratcheted up, and pulled out a crystalline block. It then raced back to Ethan and handed it to him.

The block was the size of a sugar cube. It was ruby red and pulsed like a heart.

"This volume summarizes all recent articles on glorious Project Prometheus, citizen," the librarian told him. "You will find crystal readers in the back room. Authorize data retrieval by entering your global identification number and—"

Angel stumbled into the library. She lurched and fell to one knee. She panted and clutched her side. Blood oozed between her fingers and stained her flight suit.

"I told you," Angel said, "I'd be back in a minute or two."

Ethan, Felix, and Emma ran to her.

Emma circled an arm around Angel to help steady her. She looked so fragile to Ethan.

"Just one thing went wrong . . . ," Angel said, her other knee giving out.

Felix grabbed her, too, and her eyes fluttered as she struggled to stay awake.

"That double-back trick . . . it didn't quite work out the way I wanted. They're right behind me."

"How many?" Ethan asked.

Angel whispered, "All of them."

∘ ∘ ∘ 6 ∘ ∘ ∘

RED FLARE

ETHAN RAN OUT OF THE LIBRARY. THE WALK-
ways and bridges of the city were deserted.

Angel had been mistaken—or maybe she'd hit her
head while being chased and had hallucinated the whole
thing.

But then the city shook.

Ethan's heart practically stopped as he watched a
hundred robots roll at top speed through the gate in the
outer wall. They fanned out in a half circle, casting their
supersensitive antennae back and forth. Still more robots
appeared along the top of the wall, so even if he could
make it through the city, there'd be no escaping *that* way.

He would've given his left arm for his wasp I.C.E. right now. His insect would tear those things to pieces.

Ethan reached out with his mind, trying to connect to the insect's brain like he had before—wake it and call it to him.

It was a long shot because of the distance.

He tried anyway.

That hollow, metallic feeling still filled his brain, though. Only now, the metal seemed to buzz with urgency. It drowned out whatever telepathic link he might have made to his wasp.

Ethan looked for any other way out of this jam.

Behind him, the city spiraled up—ramps and bridges and platforms—to crystalline skyscrapers in the center of the metropolis. He couldn't see any robots up there. Apparently they were all down here hunting for them.

Felix and Emma emerged from the library.

Felix carried Angel. She looked pale and could barely keep her head up.

They took in the tactical situation but said nothing.

Ethan motioned at them and pointed back into the city.

Emma and Felix, wide-eyed and probably scared out of their minds, nodded, getting that they had to leave fast . . . and in complete silence.

Felix moved out.

His sister hesitated and locked eyes with Ethan. He knew that she knew what he had to do. She could always tell when he was going to do something reckless.

"I'll be right behind you," he mouthed.

She fumed and gave him that *why is my brother crazy?* shake of her head but nonetheless ran after Felix.

Ethan dug into his pack for a signal flare.

He had to let Madison and Paul know there was trouble. Madison had to get a message back to the Seed Bank no matter what.

There were two types of flares in his pack: red and blue. Blue meant "Help needed!" Red meant "Danger!"

He pulled out a red tube with warnings printed on its side explaining which end to point where. He paused, finger wrapped around the pull cord.

Ethan really wanted to use the blue flare and call for help. But Paul would only try to fly in and end up getting the I.C.E.s blasted by the city's missile-defense system.

No. The priority had to be to warn the Seed Bank and not to send more Resister pilots here to their deaths.

He aimed the signal flare into the sky and pulled the cord.

A tremendous *whooosh* exploded from the end of the flare. Two balls of fire shot a mile into the air. Tiny parachutes deployed at the top of their trajectories and the fire hung there—brilliant and completely obvious even in full daylight.

He scanned the skies for any sign of a sleek dragonfly streaking away at supersonic speeds. Nothing.

Ethan hoped Madison had followed orders. He sighed, wondering if he'd ever see her again.

He blinked and refocused.

Every robot stopped and tracked the flares with their antennae, and then followed their twin smoky trails . . . right back to where Ethan stood.

His blood turned cold.

The robots swiveled and sped toward him.

Ethan shook off his mental vapor lock, tossed the spent flare tube, and ran for his life.

His boots pounded over metal paving stones worn smooth by countless wheel tracks. He jumped a five-foot gap in the road onto an ascending ramp.

He glanced down into that gap. It stretched as far as he could see into the gloom, revealing a huge undercity filled with churning machines, giant gears, smoking factories, and conveyor belts.

That would have been a long, long fall.

Ethan turned and sprinted up the path. His legs burned from the effort.

Dozens of robots followed to the edge—one plowed into the back of the pack and sent the lead mechanical man tumbling over and into the gap.

They reversed and backtracked, looking for another way onto the ramp he was on.

That gave Ethan a moment. He got to a platform with an obelisk monument. It was a shard of crystal that towered ten feet tall, covered with delicate mathematical equations.

He turned and scanned the city.

Felix and Emma were on a balcony three stories up.

Felix waved to him, then pointed emphatically to the left.

Ethan looked back, trying to see what Felix was pointing at, but sunlight reflected off the dome two levels down and blinded him.

He raised his hands to shield his eyes from the glare . . . and found it wasn't glare from the sun.

A cluster of robots had gathered by that dome. The bright reflection was the light of their plasma beam weapons building charge behind their helmets.

Ethan's combat reflexes kicked in.

He jumped and rolled behind the obelisk.

Multiple plasma bursts hit where he'd been standing like an idiot a split second before. Heat splashed and melted the steel subsurface and left a cooling molten crater.

White-hot panic shot through him.

These robots weren't trying to wing him and bring him in alive. They wanted to burn him to cinders!

Ethan darted up the ramp and into the shadows on the far side of a skyscraper. Scalloped columns rose around him like a redwood forest. They'd give him some cover. He weaved back and forth, running, and spotted Felix and Emma just ahead.

Felix still carried Angel, who was now limp in his arms.

Ethan jogged up to them. "Is she okay?"

Felix tensed and shifted Angel's weight. "I can't tell," he said. "She passed out. She's breathing, but still bleeding, too, Ethan."

Ethan's instinct was to help her, get his first-aid kit and patch her up. But they had to find a safe place first. Otherwise, they'd end up stabilizing Angel only to all get blasted.

"Was there any place back that way to hide?" Ethan asked.

"Hide, yes," Felix told him, "but they're dead ends."

There was no way Ethan was getting backed into a corner.

"We saw another path," Emma said. She reached up to nervously twist her braid but then stopped herself. "It goes up and through the city center. I think we could find a way into one of those big towers. At least from the top we'd be able to see what's coming after us."

Ethan laid out the tactical situation in his mind.

New Taos was a maze of steel and crystal. Skyscrapers in the center. Caves and factories underground. The Resisters were surrounded by an enemy who knew the terrain better than they did.

Felix was great at hand-to-hand combat, and Ethan and his sister were okay with the boot-camp training they'd received. The three of them combined, though, wouldn't be a match for even *one* of the hydraulically powered robots . . . and there were *hundreds* rolling around this city looking to blast them to atoms.

Unlike combat in the air, where Ethan felt he had countless ways to fight and move, his options down here were limited. None of them good.

He moved to Angel and brushed the bangs away from her closed eyes. She was breathing, but her skin was cold. He didn't like it.

They had to find a place to rest and take care of her fast.

Ethan nodded at Emma. "We'll go with your plan," he told her. "Maybe up high we can spot a way out."

Emma led them up a new path that wound around

the side of the skyscraper. "There was a wide balcony way up there," she said, starting to pant. "I thought I saw doorways into the building."

Ethan and Felix followed her up the ramp, which had no handrails. He glanced over his shoulder as they climbed higher.

From this height, New Taos looked like a platter of jewels. It was dazzling. And completely dead.

Ethan wondered what the place had been like before the Ch'zar—before the human war had turned this desert into a radioactive wasteland.

How could the people here have had so much and then thrown it all away?

They ran as fast as they could, but the steep ramp and the spent adrenaline took their toll. Ethan pumped his legs to keep going. His muscles burned and trembled. It had to be harder for Felix who, even as strong as he was, had to carry Angel.

They were all huffing and puffing as the incline leveled out to a twenty-foot-wide ledge that encircled the top of the skyscraper. They were a quarter mile up.

Ethan scanned the desert around the city. There were no vapor trails in the air. No sign of the rest of Sterling Squadron leaving the region.

There should've been something.

"We . . . can . . . rest . . . now," Emma said, totally out of breath and looking ready to collapse. She bent over for a moment, then stood and staggered toward arches that she'd thought were doors. She halted and her head dropped in dejection.

Beyond the arches weren't doors . . . but more wall.

Ethan stared.

No. There were seams in the center of the arches like maybe they were elevator doors.

Felix saw it, too. "There has to be a control panel here to open them," he said.

As if by magic, the moment he said that the doors slid apart.

Robots rolled out.

Dozens of mechanical creatures wheeled onto the balcony and surrounded them.

Ethan, Felix, and Emma went back to back. Felix clutched Angel closer to him protectively. Ethan and Emma looked at one another. There was no regret or fear in Emma's eyes—just a fierce determination that this couldn't be the end for them.

Ethan felt the same way. It couldn't end like this.

Or if it *was* the end for them, they'd go down fighting.

Together Ethan and Emma raised their hands, curled their fingers into fists, and braced.

∘ ∘ ∘ 7 ∘ ∘ ∘

BEFORE YOU GET SQUISHED

ETHAN RAISED ONE FIST TO SHIELD HIS EYES from the blinding illumination of the charging particle beams.

His lips pulled back in a snarl, but inside he trembled.

He'd faced particle beams before—even without an I.C.E.—but never so many energy beams trained on him at once.

There was nowhere to jump to, and, worse, there was no way to save his team.

He'd failed. He'd blown the mission. He'd let everyone in the Resistance down. His best friend . . .

the new recruits . . . his sister . . . they'd all depended on him.

The quavering fear inside him stilled and heated into anger: at himself.

The air rumbled and shook like thunder, like the atmosphere was going to explode around him—which might not be far from the truth when all that particle beam energy blasted him.

Instead, that thunder just got louder and louder.

It wasn't coming from the robots, because they swiveled around, aiming their antennae, trying to locate the source of the noise.

Emma and Felix took a step toward the ramp, but Ethan held up a hand, indicating they should wait. He had a feeling about this . . . and running away, well, how could they outrun those wheeled robots? They'd get picked off. One, two, three—*blammo*!

A claw gripped the edge of the balcony. It was four feet long, curved like a scythe, and ghostly green.

"No way," Emma breathed.

A titanic praying mantis climbed onto the ledge. Paul Hicks in his "Crusher" I.C.E.

Felix whooped.

The mantis swept aside three robots with one rake of

its forelimb—with so much force their steel arms wrenched and pulled out of the sockets and sent metallic bits arcing into the sky.

Ethan's snarl turned into a grin.

He had no clue how Paul had gotten here without getting blasted by the city's missile-defense system, but at the moment, he didn't care.

A housefly that weighed two tons zipped in and hovered next to the mantis. It touched down with a thud that shuddered the platform. The fly plowed into the nearest robot, throwing it so hard at the nearby robots it took off their heads and sent them skittering like soccer balls.

Emma had to dodge as one almost struck her in the chest.

The remaining robots scattered. They ignored their human opponents and re-formed to lay down overlapping fire at the I.C.E.s with their particle beams.

Two robots shot at the mantis. Paul took a direct hit on the thorax, and the exoskeleton heated, pitted, and started to melt.

The praying mantis jumped into the air, more energy beams arcing after it, but it dove low and the platform blocked their shots. Sparks fountained where the beams hit the metal and boiled away a gap in the ledge.

Lee's fly darted into the sky, zigging and zagging faster than any of the robot's beams could track him.

The robots crowded to the edge of the platform to get a better shot. More rolled out of the open elevator doorways and did the same.

They still completely ignored Ethan, Emma, and Felix.

And why not? They were no threat.

If they were ever going to run away, now was the time.

Ethan hesitated. He bristled at the notion that he was helpless. He couldn't run out in the middle of a fight— even if every opponent here outweighed him ten times over. If a few more particle beams hit Paul, he'd be too damaged to fly.

Ethan tightened his fists and charged. Emma caught on and sprinted alongside him.

They plowed into a robot in the crowd near the platform's edge—with just enough momentum to tip it over. It bumped four more, and those robots clung to six others for balance, and all eleven of the mechanical men toppled over the edge.

Emma and Ethan did a quick high five.

But then a ring of robots turned to face them.

Before they could tear Ethan and Emma apart, though,

the platform rumbled once more. Several tons of blood-red locust and silver cockroach hovered up and over the edge.

Between the two gigantic insects, they carried Felix's rhinoceros beetle, Angel's black stealth wasp, Emma's killer ladybug, and to Ethan's complete joy . . . his wasp.

They dropped the inert I.C.E.s onto the platform—crushing the robots under them.

Paul's praying mantis and Lee's housefly dove back in and blasted the remaining mechanical men with laser fire.

Grenade launchers popped open from the sides of Oliver's cockroach. There were six dull thumps, and six rocket-propelled grenades corkscrewed through the air into the open elevator doorways.

Explosions knocked Ethan onto his butt.

The elevators blew to smithereens, collapsing the side of the building. No more robots would be coming out that way.

Ethan's ears rang and blood trickled from his nose . . . but he was still grinning.

He faintly heard a sonic boom over the ringing and buzzing in his skull. Ethan turned and spotted ten miles away the signature "flower bloom" exploding cloud pattern of a subsonic-to-supersonic transition—and a torpedo-like insect on an inbound trajectory at Mach speeds.

Ethan felt his heart beat faster, imagining Madison's emerald dragonfly. The prettiest, the fastest thing in the air.

Almost the fastest.

Two dozen city-defense missiles raced after her, their exhaust trails leaving gray-white smears in the sky as they closed on Madison's position.

A position that was rapidly approaching the city.

And this skyscraper!

"Well, Lieutenant?" boomed Paul's voice from his mantis's external loudspeaker. "Get inside your suit before you get squished!"

° ° ° **8** ° ° °

OVER THE LETHAL LINE

THE WASP'S COCKPIT HISSED OPEN AS THE IN-sect seemed to invite Ethan in.

Ethan started for it, smelling the strange yet familiar burning fat, honey, and plastic scent of the cushioning gel—then he remembered Angel.

She was still out cold.

He doubled back and helped Felix get her to the black wasp. The insect glared down at them with those unnerving all-black segmented eyes, its stinger twitched, and then its cockpit hatch opened.

Ethan and Felix slid Angel inside.

The biomonitors in the cockpit flickered as Angel's

brain waves synched with the insect's mind. There was just enough contact to start the I.C.E.'s autopilot. Ethan tapped the "follow leader" icon. He took in a deep breath, held it, and then also tapped the "capture-destruct" command.

Ethan sealed her inside.

Felix and Ethan darted to their suits.

Emma was already inside her ladybug and in the air, all four tons of "cute" killer insect hovering and humming with power.

Ethan stepped into his I.C.E. The hydraulics sealed the instant his foot cleared the threshold of the cockpit. Colored lights and hexagonal displays flashed to life. Far from making Ethan feel claustrophobic, this felt natural to him, like a second skin . . . like he was part of this thing now. Weird.

More than that, he felt the blood-warm connection to the wasp's primitive mind. It was ready to dive back in— fly and fight, rend and kill.

Ethan held it back and sensed disappointment.

There'd be no hand-to-hand combat with those missiles.

He took to the air and heated the stinger laser.

Ethan was happy to be in the air once more. There was nothing like the freedom of flying.

Unfortunately, his moment of happiness faded . . .

because Angel might be dying, because his entire team might end up getting killed in the act of rescuing him.

Ethan's attention turned back to his cockpit displays: Madison's dragonfly still rocketed straight for the city.

She was a green blur . . . a vapor trail streak . . . and on her tail were two dozen silver missiles, more than enough firepower to blast her dragonfly into exoskeleton shrapnel.

Ethan tried to line up a shot with his laser, but the distance was still too far, the missiles inbound too fast to get a lock. He'd be just as likely to hit Madison.

Madison, though, seemed to have another idea.

She dove, accelerating directly toward the tallest skyscraper in the center of the city. Her approach was so low she had to weave between buildings.

In response, the missiles veered away and fanned outward, far away from where they could do harm to New Taos. It was as if they knew better.

Except one.

It must have had a lock on her heat signature or enough radiation damage to its circuits to fail on that abort order—because it stayed on Madison until its tail fin grazed a walkway, sending it tumbling into a red glass tower.

The missile detonated into a ball of fire, shattered crystal, and glittering destruction. Fractures ran down the tower all the way to its base. The structure slowly tipped

and then tottered and fell, smashing through bridges, obe-
lisks, and domes on its way. A huge plume of dust gey-
sered into the air.

Meanwhile, the missiles that had veered away exploded harmlessly high over the desert.

Ethan got it. Whatever computer intelligence ran this
city wasn't just following preprogrammed instructions. It
was smart enough to improvise and *not* blow itself up.
Mostly.

Maybe that'd give his squadron a chance to escape.

If they flew out of here now, and missiles were fired at
them, the squadron could always double back and threaten
New Taos.

He knew that . . . but would the city's controlling
computer?

There was only one way to find out.

Ethan opened the squad's short-range radio channel.
"Form up behind me and get ready on your afterburners,"
he told them.

He nervously tapped his fuel indicator: down to a
third of a tank. He'd burned up way too much in combat
to easily get back to the Seed Bank. Well, he'd worry about
that later . . . if it mattered.

Behind him, the I.C.E.s of Sterling Squadron clustered, filling the air with the thrum of insect wingbeats.

He clutched his controls. The wasp's jet engines popped out and growled with power. He poured on the speed, accelerating to four hundred miles an hour.

On his rear-facing camera, he watched the towers of New Taos get smaller and smaller.

Ten miles . . . twenty . . . and then thirty.

If the city's missile-defense system were going to blast them out of the sky again, it would've fired by now.

Maybe the city was happy to see them leave.

Ethan sure was.

New Taos had to be designated a restricted zone. No Resister could ever come back. And there was no way they could use the place as a base.

As a source of information, though, it had been a treasure trove, a glimpse of what humanity was before the Ch'zar, and sadly a glimpse of the brutal nature of human war, too.

The data crystal he'd grabbed in the library was still in his pack. Maybe it had some of the answers the Resisters wanted. Maybe it had some of the answers about his parents . . . and what was that Project Prometheus the librarian had mentioned?

Paul broke in on the squad channel. "Madison? Why'd you double back? You had specific orders."

"You had orders, too," she snapped. "I didn't see *you* stick to them."

"Yeah, well, technically I did," Paul said with his usual impervious confidence. "Ethan said not to *fly* to the city. I *walked* the I.C.E.s across the desert—started an hour after he left. Don't worry, Ethan," he said, "I let the sun heat them up to the same temperature as the desert. It was a snap. They never saw us coming on their thermals."

Ethan keyed his radio to chew Paul out—then changed his mind.

Paul *had* technically followed Ethan's orders, but he hadn't followed the intent of those orders, which was to stay safe and provide backup should Madison need it.

Considering, though, that Paul had saved their lives, Ethan let it drop this time.

Was that part of being a leader, too? Or should he discipline Paul? If he didn't, would everyone in the squadron end up doing whatever they wanted?

Apparently Madison wasn't about to let it drop.

"You're not as cool or smart as you think, Paul Hicks," she told him. "All the I.C.E.s you marched across the desert picked up ambient radiation from the dust. You guys are lighting up the Ch'zar satellite images like a Christmas tree!"

A cold dread spread from Ethan's center.

He brought up the long-range view—pictures transmitted via a hacked signal from the Ch'zar satellite network in low–Earth orbit. Their I.C.E.s looked like tiny lightning bugs on the map. They were the same color as the radiation signatures he'd seen near New Taos, although not quite at those lethal intensities.

"If *we* can see that radiation on the Ch'zar satellite network," Madison said with icy seriousness, "so can the *enemy*, you moron!"

Ethan suddenly felt like he had a target painted on his back.

He opened a private channel to Felix. "We need to get the suits scrubbed. I just hope they aren't *internally* contaminated."

"Even an external scrub won't be easy," Felix replied. "It takes more than water, Ethan. We need special soaps and rinses to remove radioactive particles from the exoskeletons."

Ethan had been afraid of that. He remembered something, though, about radiation, about cleaning it up, too. Just at the edge of his recollection.

The black stealth wasp suddenly broke formation and dove.

"What is she doing *now*?" Madison said, strangling that last word so it was more growl than language.

"Angel!" Ethan shouted over the radio. "Stay in formation!"

"Something's wrong," Emma piped in.

Maybe so, but Ethan had had it with Angel. She was completely unpredictable and a liability to the rest of the team. The instant they got back to base, he was placing her under arrest.

The black wasp landed in a boggy meadow, sinking into the mud to its first leg joint. The cockpit opened, and the insect disgorged Angel's unconscious body and then shuffled away from her as if it had a bad taste and had spit it out.

"That's just what happened to Roger," Madison whispered, horrified, over the radio.

Roger was Madison's brother. He'd hit puberty while on mission and his mind had been absorbed into the Ch'zar Collective. His wasp had rejected his controlled mind and had ejected him from its cockpit.

Just like this.

Ethan landed, jumped out of his I.C.E., and rushed to Angel.

Madison's dragonfly landed, too, but her suit didn't open. Instead, her dragonfly's laser pincers targeted Angel.

"Take it easy!" Ethan told Madison.

He knelt next to Angel. She was out cold. Still breathing, though.

Could the Ch'zar take over an unconscious mind?

Emma and Felix landed in the field. They exited their suits and ran to him. Paul, Lee, Oliver, and Kristov touched down and crowded by them, too.

Emma took Angel's wrist to check her pulse. She gasped as she stared at Angel's radiation counter.

Ethan's heart skipped a beat.

The counter's indicator was five ticks *past* the fatal dosage line.

"It must have happened in the junkyard," Emma whispered as the color drained from her face. "When the robots were after her, I bet she stumbled into a hot spot."

Kristov looked helpless and wrung his hands.

"That's why the wasp rejected her," Felix said. "Her body is like poison inside the suit."

Despite all the crazy stuff she'd done, despite that he'd just promised himself he'd throw her in the Seed Bank brig when they got back, Ethan would have done anything to save her.

But Angel was going to die.

Madison finally slipped out of her dragonfly. She came

over and glanced at Angel, Emma, and the radiation counter. The anger vanished from her pointed features.

"I'm sorry," Madison said. "There's one more piece of bad news, Lieutenant."

"It can wait," Ethan said a little too abruptly. "We can't fly Angel back to the base, so we need to get a message to them. Madison, open an encrypted channel to Colonel Winter."

"We can't," Madison said. "That's what I was about to tell you. I've been trying to contact the Seed Bank since New Taos. The Ch'zar have jammed all frequencies—even the emergency bands."

"They've never been able to do that before," Felix said, standing and frowning.

"I know," Madison whispered. "Either they're targeting the Seed Bank transceivers or they're burning enough power to blank the entire region."

Ethan chewed his lip. He just *had* to talk to Dr. Irving.

He was on his own, though.

There must be another way to help Angel—something out here he could use to slow the radiation poisoning in her and get it off their suits.

Ethan dug into his flight suit and pulled out the map. He zoomed out so he could see the southeastern portion of North America. With less than a quarter tank of jet fuel left in their I.C.E.s, they didn't have much range at decent speed.

Then he spotted a green splotch on the map and remembered something.

Radiation.

It was a long shot. A complete gamble.

But a chance nonetheless.

"I know a place we can clean our suits. A place where we can get Angel help, too."

Madison sidled closer to look at what he was staring at on the map. Her eyes widened. "You can't be serious," she said.

"Totally serious."

Ethan pointed at the dot centered on his map.

The label beneath the dot read SANTA BLANCA.

∘ ∘ ∘ 9 ∘ ∘ ∘

COMMAND HEADACHES

ETHAN SAT IN THE PASSENGER SEAT OF A
Blanca Dairy delivery truck. He had an extreme feeling of
déjà vu. He'd been inside a truck like this just a few
months ago—kidnapped by Madison and Felix after his
last soccer game.

He grimaced at how innocent he'd been, worrying
about getting into high school, for crying out loud, instead
of realizing that he had to save the world.

Tonight everything was different.

Including the fact that he smelled like old banana
peels and rotten tomatoes. His flight suit needed a bath in

the worst way. At least it was covered with a milk delivery person's white coveralls.

Emma was in back, perched on a milk crate and intently staring out the front, as if this were the first time she'd seen the pastures outside Santa Blanca.

In a way, she *was* seeing them for the first time, seeing the place for what it really was. Santa Blanca was a rural township full of happy families and surrounded by farmlands and mountains.

It was also a prison where kids like them were raised to join a race of mind-controlled slaves when they hit puberty. A place where no one knew the truth.

Madison drove. Of the three of them, she was the only one who knew how to drive a car. The steering wheel was huge in her tiny hands, but she expertly handled the vehicle, speeding along the moonlit road at nearly twice the posted speed limit.

Emma moved up and nudged Ethan's shoulder. "Tell me again why we didn't bring Felix?" she asked.

Ethan shook his head, wondering if Emma had a crush on the big guy. She was a year older than him, one year closer to puberty . . . and a year closer to the end of her aboveground activities.

"Felix and Paul know the cleaning protocols for the

I.C.E. suits," he said. "They need to direct the others. It's a huge job, and they're the only ones able to pull off that part of the mission tonight."

Ethan missed having Felix around. He knew he could always depend on him.

Which is exactly why he'd put him in charge of that part of the plan—Ethan's "brilliant" plan that he'd dreamed up on the flight into Santa Blanca.

He shifted in the tattered seat, uncomfortable about how much was at risk.

They'd flown straight for Santa Blanca and landed near the dump far from the city. Ethan wasn't sure how well the Ch'zar could track their radiation-contaminated suits, so they had to move fast. Sterling Squadron had then "liberated" a few trash trucks. They'd loaded the I.C.E.s inside the cavernous metal bellies of the vehicles. That would hide most of the radiation on the suits.

He hoped.

"I get that we need some antiradiation treatment," Emma whispered, "but was *this* the only place? I mean, won't they know us in Santa Blanca?"

"Ch'zar-controlled adults would recognize us *anywhere*," Ethan told her. He suppressed a shudder just thinking about this. "If one of them here sees our faces, the entire alien hive mind will remember us and respond. They'll send everyone in the city after us. We'll have to be supercareful."

"Getting our I.C.E.s back to Santa Blanca is our only choice," Madison said, and looked over at Emma instead of watching the road, which drove Ethan crazy every time she did it. "If your brother is right and there are antiradiation chemicals here, Felix and Paul can get the suits cleaned, and the squadron will be back in business."

"The chemicals are here," Ethan assured them. "Along with showers to clean up malfunctioning athletic suits. Our I.C.E.s are bigger, but it'll work."

That's what Ethan had been trying to remember before. Earlier this year, an athletic suit had had a reactor breach. The hazardous materials team from the fire department came and set up huge showers and doused the suit with chemicals. Coach Norman told him the hazmat team had special rinses that captured and washed off radioactive particles.

Felix and Paul and the rest of Sterling Squadron were driving their commandeered trash trucks right now to the Santa Blanca firehouse to find a way to secretly "borrow" those showers and chemicals. At least, that was the plan.

"I'm worried about the radiation on our suits," Emma

said, irritation creeping into her tone. "But I'm more worried about finding a treatment for *Angel*."

"Oh . . . her," Madison replied, and looked back at the road.

Of course, Angel . . . Ethan was so worried for her.

"This is the best chance we have to save Angel," he said, keeping his voice steady, although he felt a choking in his throat, remembering how she had been so limp and lifeless after her wasp had spit her out.

"The Resisters and the Ch'zar have similar technologies, but they're not identical," Ethan went on. "Dr. Irving said he borrowed a lot of their tech to make our I.C.E.s. We use old human technology, though, especially in our medicine. The Ch'zar might have another way to deal with radiation. They've collected science from a dozen other species in the galaxy."

"So we're going to just sneak into Santa Blanca General Hospital and hope we find something," Madison murmured, unconvinced.

"You have a better plan?" Ethan asked.

She shrugged. "It'll work, Lieutenant. Piece of cake. Angel gets her skinny little neck saved and the Resistance gets more effective antiradiation medicine—what's not to like?"

Madison wouldn't meet his glare. There was an edge to her words that Ethan did not like one bit.

He half suspected if it were up to Madison, she'd actually let Angel *die*.

What if that was the correct command decision? Was Ethan soft for risking everyone's life to save one team member? And the most troublesome team member at that?

Maybe . . . but it was the only way he could operate as a commander.

He would have done it for *any* person in his squad, but like Angel said, he and she were both "different."

Emerson's gas station was ahead. It was closed for the evening, but Madison pulled up to a pump anyway.

She hopped out, ripped off the panel of the gas pump, got it to work, and started filling the milk truck's tank.

"I want a full tank," she told him, "in case we have to make a break for it."

Ethan nodded, although he wasn't sure where they'd run to if there was trouble. Without I.C.E. suits that the Ch'zar couldn't track . . . without a way to contact the Seed Bank . . . they might be stuck here for a long time.

Ethan turned to talk to Emma, but he stopped because she had both palms pressed to her forehead in obvious pain.

"You okay?" he whispered.

"Headache," she murmured. "I felt something like this

back in New Taos . . . only it was a little buzzing, and *this* is more like a hammer of pounding blood. It's hard to explain."

She looked up. Her dark eyes were glassy, her forehead creased with tension.

He reached out to pat her on the arm. He was going to suggest that she grab some aspirin from the first-aid kits, but when he touched her, Ethan felt what she felt, too.

It was like the pulses of a hundred other people thundering in his head. The pressure was intense.

He let go and sat up straighter, both hands involuntarily rising to his head to put pressure on the pain.

Was his sister being affected by the Ch'zar mental domination? She was technically old enough to hit puberty. It wasn't like puberty was a switch, though, that just got flipped. The physical changes could take months to completely manifest.

Dr. Irving had told him there was a critical point, however, when the chemistry in the brain changed. When Madison's brother, Roger, was taken over, it was only a matter of minutes.

"It's not that," Emma told him. "It's not like I can't push the feeling out when I concentrate."

It bugged Ethan that she could so easily guess what he was thinking.

Was that a symptom of a Ch'zar hive mind?

No . . . he didn't think so. He and Emma had always been able to guess the other's thoughts most of the time.

He took a deep breath and tried not to freak out.

"Let me know if it gets any worse, okay?" he said.

She locked eyes with him. The pain eased from her gaze, and the tension on her face smoothed. She slugged him—hard—in the shoulder. "You'll be the second to know." She snorted a quick laugh. "I'll be fine. Worry about more important things."

Ethan relaxed a little but wasn't entirely convinced his sister was 100 percent okay.

He knew one thing, though: with Angel's deadly radiation poisoning, the alien-controlled adults of Santa Blanca who could recognize them at a glance, and his sister acting "quirky," the clock was ticking.

It was only a matter of time before *something* went very wrong.

The gas tank of the milk truck gurgled and overflowed.

"Done," Madison chirped. She hopped back into the milk truck and they sped off.

They approached the edge of Santa Blanca. Things were different in his former home from the last time Ethan was here. The normal warm streetlights had been replaced with tall banks of lights mounted on cranes that cast harsh illumination over entire city blocks.

It was bright enough to see that on every corner, two adults in green Neighborhood Watch jackets stood on lookout.

Emma tossed Madison a Blanca Dairy jacket and cap.

"Take the wheel," Madison told Ethan.

He did, and she shrugged on the jacket and cap, pulling the hat low so no one could see her face. She then grabbed the wheel back.

Ethan slumped into the passenger seat.

They drove ahead . . . right past the adults.

He peeked through the window. The adults didn't give them a second glance.

Posters covered the brick walls of Barker's Drugstore and the public library.

One poster showed an adult kneeling next to some kids. They all smiled. Under this was the caption:

OBEY

On another poster, there were a pair of blue eyes and the words:

WE'RE WATCHING FOR *YOUR* PROTECTION

A third poster had a father and a mother holding a baby in their arms, both cooing at it. The poster read:

YOUR PARENTS KNOW BEST

But next to this one on the brick wall was spray-painted:

LɪE!

The paint still looked wet and drippy.

"What's going on here?" Madison whispered.

"I don't know . . . ," Ethan whispered back.

He had a vague idea, though.

Before he'd joined the Resisters, he'd returned to Santa Blanca in his wasp to rescue his sister. He'd failed, but there'd been a titanic battle between him and the Ch'zar at Northside Elementary School. Felix and Madison had flown back to help and together they'd *totaled* the school.

Everyone in Santa Blanca had to have seen it.

There was no way the adults could've covered it up.

That's why everything was different—the normal, happy township had to have more rules, more authority . . . because how would you even start to explain to the kids here how giant bugs had torn apart their school?

Every kid would have to be kept under tight control until they were part of the Ch'zar hive mind.

Ethan felt like throwing up. *He'd* caused this trouble.

"Good," Emma said, climbing up front. "At least they've seen the truth, right? Look over there."

She pointed to five kids at the mouth of an alley. There were no adults on the corner, and the kids were spray-painting a frowning face over a poster that read:

ALL RULES ARE GOOD RULES

"*Not* so good," Madison muttered, and looked to her right.

She slowed the truck and nodded to the end of Main Street and then down intersecting Pine Street. From either side, four adults in Neighborhood Watch jackets moved at a fast walk toward the kids, who hadn't spotted them.

Ethan hesitated, uncertain what to do.

He had his own life-or-death mission to carry out. He couldn't get involved in this mess, too.

But wasn't it his fault all this was happening?

He weighed what was more important—getting Angel

the antiradiation medicine, getting back to the Seed Bank, or saving these kids here and now.

Ethan swallowed, but his throat stayed dry.

He decided.

He'd let Colonel Winter make the big strategic calls. Ethan couldn't let these kids get caught.

"Step on it," he ordered Madison. "Get to them before those adults can catch them."

Madison's lips formed a grim flat line. She stomped on the gas pedal; the back wheels spun, then grabbed, and the milk truck shot forward.

∘ ∘ ∘ 10 ∘ ∘ ∘

GRIZZLIES REUNION

THE MILK TRUCK SLID SIDEWAYS TO A HALT, AL-most crashing *into* the group of kids.

They stood there, dumbfounded, staring into the headlights like idiots.

Ethan couldn't believe it. They had plenty of room to jump out of the way. They could have run down the alley or kicked open the side door to the library and escaped.

What was wrong with them?

What was wrong was that they weren't Resisters. Weren't used to combat conditions. In other words, they were normal.

The problem with being "normal" was that in the real

world, it could get you killed. Or, at the very least, doom you to becoming part of a mind-controlled slave race.

The kids weren't *completely* clueless, though.

Bandannas covered their faces. They had on gloves, too, so paint wouldn't get on their fingers.

They were sneaky, at least. That was something.

Emma opened the truck's side door and motioned for the five to climb inside. "Hurry up," she said. "Those adults will be here any second."

That got their attention. They looked up and down the street and saw the Neighborhood Watch running toward them. The five kids stumbled and pushed their way into the truck.

Madison didn't wait for the door to shut. She slammed the accelerator and the truck screamed down the road—straight at the group of adults.

They dove into the gutter.

"Madison!" Ethan cried.

"No worries, Lieutenant," she told him, and her crooked smile appeared. "They moved."

Ethan turned to reassure the kids they'd rescued. His mouth dropped open, though, because—bandannas over their faces or not—Ethan recognized the Grizzlies-team letterman jacket and the curly black hair of his soccer teammate, Bobby Buckman.

Bobby's eyes widened as he took in Ethan's features. Ethan had dropped a few pounds and was leaner and meaner than he'd ever been at Santa Blanca.

"Ethan?" Bobby pulled off his bandanna. He turned to the other kids. "It's him," he whispered. "The one they said died in the Geo Transit Tunnel disaster." He turned back to Ethan. "But you didn't. . . . You got away, didn't you?"

Madison burned rubber around the corner. She pulled under the awning of the Spitfire Hamburger drive-through. "Talk later," she said. "We've got to ditch this truck and find another vehicle. Their cameras are everywhere and spotted us for sure."

"Cameras?" Bobby asked. "What cameras?"

Ethan frowned. He'd totally forgotten about the cameras the Ch'zar had hidden all over Santa Blanca. When Coach Norman had tried to interrogate Ethan, he'd shown Ethan pictures taken of him on the streets—even inside his house.

"Is there a place we can hide?" Ethan asked Bobby.

Bobby frowned and looked back and forth among his co-conspirators. They all nodded.

"Okay," Bobby whispered to Ethan. "I'll take a chance and trust you." There was a threatening edge to his words.

It was a strange thing, because Bobby Buckman had trusted Ethan his entire life. But Ethan could also understand how everything was different now. How when your whole world started tilting sideways . . . you didn't know what or who to trust . . . even yourself.

They clambered out of the milk truck.

"This way," Bobby said, and he sprinted into the shadows.

They hopped over a fence and cut through a backyard, darting into the apple orchard in Evergreen Park. Moonlight made long, eerie shadows as the kids wordlessly slinked under the swaying branches.

Ethan hesitated.

Just two blocks away was his old house. Was someone else living there now? It hurt to think about that.

Emma caught up to him and set her hand on his back. "Don't," she whispered, so softly he barely heard her. There was pain in her voice, so he knew she was feeling the same thing he was: they missed their parents.

He moved on.

Bobby ducked into a backyard. Weeds had overgrown a tomato garden, and the house was completely dark.

"This one is empty," Bobby whispered back at Ethan. "We've been using it for our secret meetings."

An empty house? Santa Blanca didn't have empty houses. There was one house for every large, happy family.

Ethan wanted to ask Bobby a million questions, but before he could, Bobby and the others slipped through an open window. They skulked into the basement, and Bobby snapped on the lights.

Ethan saw that the tiny basement windows had been painted black so no one could see inside.

The other kids pulled the bandannas off their faces. Ethan knew them all from his soccer team: George, Sara, Leo, and James.

He hardly recognized them. They looked older. They looked like they'd been through a lot.

Madison crossed her arms over her chest. "Oh boy, are we going to go through this whole 'I don't believe the world's been invaded' thing, Blackwood? We're racing the clock."

Ethan was going to tell her to have a little sympathy for these guys, but she was right. Every minute they spent here was a minute stolen from Angel and the rest of the team, who were depending on them.

"You don't have to spell everything out for us." Bobby suddenly looked sick and pale. "We pieced together a few things. Our parents are . . . well, something is wrong with them. And those bugs . . ."

Ethan sat on a pile of newspapers. The other kids settled around him—except Madison, who checked that the windows were locked.

"This is going to sound nuts," Ethan said, "even if you have a few of the pieces already."

Ethan started with how the entire world, this place, the history they'd been taught in school—it was all a lie.

They nodded.

Ethan told them about World War IV and how humanity almost killed itself—how the Ch'zar invaded and won by mind-controlling every adult on the planet.

He cast a split-second meaningful glance at Emma and Madison as he purposely left out how Dr. Irving and a few other adults escaped by being far underground in the Seed Bank.

There were secrets . . . and then there were *secrets*.

"Mind-controlled adults," Bobby said, fidgeting. "You mean our parents, too?"

"Yeah," Ethan said.

The kids considered that a moment. Ethan could almost see them connect their parents' weird behavior, the way all the adults seemed to act as one at times, and the new rules.

"Does that mean they don't love us?" Leo asked.

Madison glanced at her wristwatch and made a hurry-up signal at Ethan.

Madison had parents and grandparents—all Resisters in control of their own minds. Sure, her life was no party, but at least she never had to deal with not knowing if she'd been loved or lied to all her life.

Thankfully, Emma took over the awkward moment. "We don't know," she told him. "Maybe the Ch'zar have feelings for us. It's probably not like we think of normal emotions, though."

This was harder than Ethan had thought it would be. All the feelings he had for his parents, feelings he thought he'd gotten a handle on, started to well up.

Did his parents still love him?

Tears blurred his eyes. He blinked them quickly away.

They had to. They had to be different like he and Emma were different. There was no way they were part of the Ch'zar Collective.

He clung to that belief.

But as for the other kids . . . there was far less hope for their parents.

It would be the hardest truth they would ever have to accept.

Ethan went on, talking about the Ch'zar—how they

used Santa Blanca to raise kids until they hit puberty, then sent them off to high school where they joined the collective mind, how the aliens were stripping the natural resources of the planet to build ships to seed the galaxy, and how they'd mutated insects into giant biomechanical fighting and flying machines called I.C.E. suits.

A long silence followed Ethan's short history.

"It makes sense," George said. The pain was thick in his voice.

"We've seen a few of them," Bobby added, "flying over at night. Locusts, I think, but as big as trucks. It started after the school burned down. A lot of kids got sick and were shipped off to Haven Heart for treatment. None of them have come back."

He sounded scared. Ethan didn't blame him.

Emma and Ethan shared a glance, knowing that those kids wouldn't ever be coming back. It was how the Ch'zar were controlling the situation. It was the reason this house was empty.

"A few of us on the team got together to share what we knew," Bobby continued. "All of our parents started acting supernice . . . but then all these new rules came down, and more people started disappearing. We knew something was rotten, just not . . . this."

"We can help," Ethan said consolingly.

Madison rolled her eyes.

He knew she was right, that taking on more problems was crazy, but Ethan felt an obligation to his former team-mates.

"But first we need help," Ethan said. "We have a sick friend and need to break into the hospital to get the right medicine."

Bobby considered, then brightened and turned toward Sara. "Your mom's a doctor, isn't she? What do you know about the hospital?"

Ethan exhaled. Bobby was a true buddy. He wasn't asking who or why; he just wanted to help.

For a moment, Ethan felt like he was back on the soccer field, his old team around him, huddled together, coming up with a crazy plan to win the game.

He could almost believe they'd all get out of this in one piece.

"If you want to sneak into the hospital," Sara explained, "the best way is the laundry service. Those guys make deliveries to every floor, and they're always wearing surgical masks to avoid infection."

Madison smiled so broadly her pointed face dimpled. "Perfect," she said. "Blackwood, these guys are okay."

Floodlights snapped on outside. They were so bright that streams of illumination shot through spots on the window the black paint hadn't entirely covered. Light streamed through the floorboards overhead, too.

A voice boomed over a loudspeaker:

"Kids, we know you're in there. Come out or we'll be forced to come and get you!"

Ethan's blood ran cold, pure liquid nitrogen freezing cold . . . because that voice was Coach Norman's.

○ ○ ○ **11** ○ ○ ○

TEAM MUTINY

THE KIDS FROM THE GRIZZLIES SOCCER TEAM froze. They'd been trained to obey Coach Norman.

Not Ethan.

He'd seen the man for what he really was. Coach Norman had tried to interrogate and torture Ethan and inject him with chemicals that would accelerate the puberty process.

Coach Norman was the enemy.

Ethan ran up the basement stairs and slammed the dead bolt on the door. He raced back down to secure the windows, but Madison had already done it.

"Eight adults on this side of the house," she reported,

. **105** .

peering through an unpainted pinhole in the window. "*Not* the Neighborhood Watch either. They're in riot armor, carrying shields and batons."

Emma cast about, looking for weapons. She found a bag of golf clubs, pulled out a driver, and experimentally hefted it. "They must've seen us if they're dressed for a fight."

"I don't think so," Ethan whispered. "If they saw *us,* they'd be here in Ch'zar I.C.E.s."

The Resisters shared a glance. They'd outwitted the Ch'zar too many times to expect anything but a lethal response . . . unless the enemy was going easy because of the other kids here.

"They've come for us," Bobby whispered. The fear on his face hardened into determination and pride. "We stopped a bus full of 'sick' kids a few days ago. After what you just told us, Ethan, I guess that was the right thing to do. I think we made enough of a difference for them to take us seriously."

Coach Norman's voice boomed once more over the loudspeaker: "*Kids, you broke a few rules, but you just got some bad information. There are a lot of rumors being spread out there. No one is going to blame you. Come out now and there'll be no marks on your permanent record.*"

Most of the Santa Blanca kids flinched at that last comment and took tentative steps toward the stairs.

Bobby hissed at them, "Are you guys crazy?"

They looked confused and ashamed.

In a way they *were* crazy. They'd been told for the last ten years that getting into high school was the one thing they had to do. Good grades, extracurricular activities, brushing your teeth—obeying. It's what every parent was supposed to teach their kids. But it was part of the Ch'zar plan.

"The only permanent record you guys are going to have is joining the Ch'zar as mindless drones. Snap out of it!" Madison said.

"Bobby?" A woman's worried voice came over the loudspeaker next. *"It's Mom, Bobby. We're not going to blame you, honey. Just come out. It'll be okay."*

Bobby crumpled in slow motion like he'd been punched in the gut. He shook his head. "Ethan," he whispered. "I can't. That's my mom. She can't be . . ."

Ethan moved to Bobby and held him up. "It's *not* your mom," he said. "At least not the mom you think she is." He held Bobby's gaze.

Bobby wavered, looking at Ethan, and then he glanced at the windows.

Ethan felt sorry for him. It was too much for *anyone* to believe. How could a person not love their mom and dad? Ethan hadn't been able to swallow the story about the Ch'zar and their mind control—even *after* he'd seen the I.C.E.s up close and personal. He'd wanted it all to be just a bad dream.

"*George!*" a man's voice shouted over the loudspeaker. "*Get out right now! Stop all this nonsense!*"

George was the defensive lead for the Grizzlies. He was a big kid.

He jumped up at the sound of his dad's angry voice as if he'd been slapped in the face. He moved toward the door. "Sorry, guys," he said. "I just don't believe my dad is controlled by some bug."

In a heartbeat, Madison got ahead of him and held up her hand. "Don't," she told him.

"Step aside, little girl," George snorted.

That was the wrong thing to say to Madison.

She jabbed him in the solar plexus twice and followed up with a punch to the nose.

George staggered back, tears streaming from his eyes. "Hey!"

"I could've *broken* your nose, buddy," Madison said with a cruel smile, "along with a few ribs. Care to try your luck again on this 'little girl'?"

"Sara . . . ?" A woman's voice hiccuped with sobs over the loudspeaker. *"Please, baby, we're here to help you. You're sick."*

Sara clutched at her stomach as she listened to her mom.

Overhead, floorboards creaked and Ethan heard soft footfalls. He grabbed Bobby's arm. "Is there another way out of this place?"

The situation was explosive. James and George looked like they wanted to bolt for the basement door and give up. The Resisters looked ready for a fight (adults in riot gear notwithstanding). And the rest of his old team—Sara, Leo, and Bobby—looked like they didn't trust anyone at this point, not even themselves.

"Is there a way out?" Ethan said again, shaking Bobby.

"Yeah," Bobby said, snapping out of his trance. "There's a side door, but it's locked with a padlock on the outside." He glanced in the corner, shaking his head. "There's a storm grate . . . but that just leads to the sewer."

"Sewer tunnels," Emma said, like someone might say, "Thanks for the wonderful birthday gift!"

For a girl who prided herself on her appearance, making sure her makeup was just right, that her braid was neat and tight, Emma showed no hesitation in prying open the sewer grate with her golf club. She couldn't help but wrinkle her freckled nose at the scent wafting up, though.

"It's good," she said with a cough. "Stinky, but big enough to get through. There's even a ladder."

The doorknob on the basement door jiggled.

Then everything happened at once.

George and James made a break for the door, tromping up the stairs.

Ethan guessed they were unable to handle the truth, unwilling to believe their parents didn't love them.

"You idiots! Don't!" Bobby screamed, and started after them.

Sara and Leo looked too scared to make a move.

Emma took in the situation, glanced once at Ethan and Madison, and then went down the ladder into the sewer tunnels. Ethan knew she'd scout ahead and make sure it was safe.

Madison moved over the tunnel, hands raised, ready to cover their escape . . . or if necessary, to take on all comers in a fight for her life.

And Ethan? He wanted to save the lives of his *former* teammates and get out of here alive with his *current* teammates.

Madison darted over to him, grabbed his hand, and yanked him to the storm drain.

Meanwhile, the basement door burst inward. Adults in padded armor and boots, holding shields and batons, tried to push through and down the stairs, while George and James were trying to get out to meet their parents. It was complete chaos as the kids shoved past the adults and the adults went over the kids—and they all ended up in a heap at the bottom of the stairs.

Ethan looked at the storm drain. The cast-iron rectangle was just big enough to let him squeeze through. Oddly, there were ladder rungs descending into the darkness like Emma had said. Why would anyone put a ladder to the sewer in their basement?

He tested the first rung with his foot. It was solid.

He stepped down three more so he was half in and half out of the hole.

"Hurry," Madison hissed. "I'll be right behind you."

Two adults in riot gear managed to get to their feet.

Bobby, Sara, and Leo seemed to wake up then. They tackled the adults from the side and dog-piled on top of them.

"Go!" Bobby shouted. "Now!"

Ethan started back up. He wasn't abandoning anyone in a fight.

"I've got this," Madison said. She placed her boot on his shoulder and pushed.

Ethan's hands and feet slipped off the wet rungs. He fell through the air, scraping walls, and hit a concrete floor.

Overhead, there were shouts and screams, the crack of wood . . . or it might have been bone.

A beam of light cut through the darkness, momentarily dazzling Ethan, then moved to the side.

Emma held a flashlight, shining it back and forth, revealing a moss-covered tunnel five feet wide. Cables and pipes ran along the walls, and a water-filled channel cut through the center of the floor.

"These are more than sewer tunnels," she whispered. She glanced up at the opening above.

Shadowy figures appeared and clambered down the ladder. First Bobby, followed in rapid succession by Leo and Sara.

"Where are the others?" Emma asked. "Where's Madison?"

Bobby shook his head. "I . . . I don't know."

Ethan grabbed the rungs. He had to get Madison.

But then he saw someone jump into the hole.

He dodged aside.

Madison—sliding down with both hands and feet braced against the walls—landed in a crouch where he had been a moment ago.

There was a flash and boom from the basement that

left Ethan's ears ringing. Boxes and shelves and crates crashed over the storm drain.

"Flash-bang grenade," Madison explained. "They'll be disoriented for a few minutes, so let's make it count, Lieutenant."

Ethan noticed that when she called him Lieutenant (not Ethan or Blackwood), he usually had some difficult command decision to make . . . like she used his rank to remind him of that.

He stared up at the dust and the sealed storm grate.

There was no way to go back and fight now.

There was only one way to save his former teammates—get the I.C.E. suits up and running.

"Let's move out," Ethan said, and ran into the dark.

°°°12°°°

THE BLOOD MUSIC

ETHAN WASN'T SURE HOW FAR THEY'D RUN. HE was still thinking about the kids he'd left behind. Thinking, too, about how Angel was doing. Wondering if Felix and Paul and the others had found what they needed to get the I.C.E.s cleaned.

And in the back of his head, there was a nagging suspicion that there was *more* to worry about—especially how the Ch'zar had been able to blanket-jam the Seed Bank's emergency broadcast bands.

Something felt *very* wrong about that.

"Hang on," Madison said, and grabbed Ethan's elbow. She flipped open her wristwatch/radiation counter to use the built-in compass. "West is that way." She pointed left. "That's the direction of the hospital."

Ethan checked his mental map of Santa Blanca. Madison was right.

"Hospital?" Bobby slumped against the wall and slid down to his knees. He looked exhausted and disoriented.

"We still have to get that medicine for our sick friend," Ethan explained.

Bobby shook his head.

Ethan wasn't sure if he was disagreeing about their priorities or if he was in denial about the entire world.

Emma knelt next to Bobby and set her hand on his shoulder. "It's going to be okay."

"How can you say that?" Leo asked. Leo was the goalkeeper on the Grizzlies and had wanted to be an architect when he went off to high school. He was always building model dams and bridges. "My mom and dad aren't what I thought they were. This whole place . . ." Leo waved around in a hopeless, helpless gesture, unable to find the words.

"Is a lie?" Ethan offered.

"That's exactly it," Sara said. "And if *everything* is a lie, what does *anything* matter?"

"They're losing it," Madison whispered to Ethan.

Ethan had similarly "lost it" the first time he'd seen the

truth. Although that first time turned into an I.C.E.–enemy robot smashup, so it was either cope with the situation or get squished.

In some ways that had been a lot easier than this.

"Let's take a minute to get our heads together," Ethan said.

The Resisters dug through their packs and passed around canteens and protein bars.

As they munched in silence, Emma examined the walls in detail with her flashlight. She motioned for Ethan and pointed. Some pipes and cables had tendrils and side branches that looked like veins. Emma moved her flashlight aside and the organic parts glowed for a moment before fading.

"Bioluminescence," she said. "Odds are that's Ch'zar engineering."

Ethan would never get used to the mix of bio- and mechanical technologies—even if he did admire his own wasp I.C.E. suit. It was still gross.

"I bet the adults use these tunnels to move through Santa Blanca when they don't want to be noticed," he said. "Or when they have to move something alien. Or maybe even the Ch'zar themselves come through these tunnels."

The kids stopped eating and glanced down the tunnel,

looking and straining to hear something besides their own thumping heartbeats.

"What do they look like?" Bobby whispered. "I mean, the aliens who're supposed to be in charge of every-thing?"

Ethan turned to Madison to see if she knew. She shrugged.

"We've never seen one," Madison told them. "They send out robots and I.C.E.s—those giant insect battle suits you've seen—and use mind-controlled people, but we've never had a confirmed report of them coming down from their spaceships in orbit."

Ethan shuddered, remembering how they'd *almost* seen a Ch'zar. There was probably one on the command zeppelin that directed the attack force searching for the Seed Bank last month. They'd blasted that zeppelin out of the air, and then every enemy I.C.E. had dived into the flaming wreckage and died in a futile attempt to save some *thing* inside.

Later, Ch'zar ships came and removed the smoldering wreckage . . . so the Resisters never found out for sure.

"You've never seen them?" Bobby asked, pressing his hands to his temples. "How do you know they even exist?"

Ethan sighed. Bobby still struggled with the truth. He didn't blame him.

Ethan was about to tell him how Coach Norman had told him about the Ch'zar and showed him holograms of their mother ship in orbit, but Emma spoke first.

"Look." Emma pulled Bobby to his feet and showed him the veinlike structures on the wall. "Does that look like anything a human could make?"

"No . . . ," Bobby admitted, squirming, half fascinated, half repulsed.

Emma reached out with her hand and hovered over the veins. "Try this," she whispered. "You can actually *feel* them."

"No way," Bobby breathed.

Emma locked eyes with Ethan.

He had a sinking feeling he knew what she meant. He didn't want to try it . . . but he didn't want to look like a big chicken either. So he held out his hand, too, almost touching the organic structures on the wall.

He felt a faster pulse inside the things.

His own pulse accelerated to match the elevated beat. Then he felt more—a dozen other beats, hundreds, thousands, all thumping away; it was a concert, beautiful music that filled his mind and flesh.

Something far away directed the blood music.

The Ch'zar Collective, just a hairsbreadth from his fingertips.

All he had to do was reach out . . . and connect.

He jerked his hand back, horrified.

Emma kept her hand where it was, then moved it a smidgen nearer to the wall. "They're looking for us," she said, and closed her eyes. "I can hear them whispering our names."

"You can *what?*" Madison said, her eyes widening.

Emma ignored Madison, and her eyes opened and locked with Ethan's. "They didn't see us—I mean the Resisters—in the basement. They know some of us are here, though. They detected our I.C.E.s inbound and are looking for them . . . on the outskirts of town. They don't have a clue they're smack in the middle of Santa Blanca in trash trucks."

Ethan grabbed his sister's wrist and pulled her hand away from the wall.

"Don't do that," he told her.

Madison made a click with her tongue, getting Ethan's attention. Her pixie features bunched with extreme concern.

Ethan could guess what Madison was thinking. He was thinking the same thing.

Emma was a year older than they were. Thirteen . . . and maybe changing—puberty and the huge shift in brain chemistry that went with it—and that'd make her vulnerable to Ch'zar mental domination. Here in the middle of enemy territory, there was nothing they could do about it either.

Emma looked at Madison and him and laughed.

It startled Ethan and he dropped her wrist.

"There's no way I'm getting absorbed, you two," Emma said. "I'm just smarter than you, Ethan, so I can hear a little bit more. It's not like I *want* to dive in deeper."

Madison's brow knit in confusion at this.

But Ethan got it. He'd experienced the same thing before in his wasp I.C.E. suit—that melded-mind feeling, sinking in, like he was becoming part of that insect brain . . . but also repulsed by the "otherness" of it all.

Madison gazed at them both, licked her lips, and then slowly said, "Maybe we just better get moving."

Ethan stared at his sister, unsure if she was okay or not.

"Don't be stupid," Emma told him. She slugged him in his shoulder with her usual knuckle-grinding strength.

"Ow! Okay," Ethan said. He grabbed his backpack. "Come on, guys," he said, and motioned to the rest of the Grizzlies.

"I can't . . . ," Bobby said.

"You've got to believe us by now," Emma said.

"I do," Bobby replied, and let out a tremendous sigh. "I know you're right." He swallowed, choking back a sob, then cleared his throat. "That's why I've got to go *back*."

Ethan didn't understand. Was he going back to his parents? Giving up? That didn't sound like the Bobby he knew.

"I have to try and save the others," Bobby explained. "They're going to be taken on those buses for 'sick' kids. We'll never see them again."

"Yeah . . . ," Madison whispered. "You probably won't."

"We've got to stop that," Bobby said to his teammates. Sara and Leo nodded back to him.

"Come on, Ethan," he said. "We can do this if we stick together."

Bobby was talking as if this were a team huddle in some soccer game.

Ethan tried to see how they could pull it off. Sabotage the buses first, stage some diversion, get the kids out, maybe into these tunnels . . . but then what?

Did it matter what came next? He could figure that part out as they went. The important thing was saving the rest of the kids in Santa Blanca.

What if the Ch'zar took them to Sterling? What if they took them straight to Ward Zero? Or just drugged them until they grew up, and "installed" them in enemy I.C.E.s?

There was no way he was letting *that* happen.

"Lieutenant . . . ," Madison said, and gently set her

hand on his arm. There was an uncharacteristic look of sympathy in her eyes, along with the expectation that he was going to give orders—the *right* orders.

The responsibility that Colonel Winter had given him tightened like a noose around his neck.

He had to finish his mission. He had to get back to the Seed Bank and deliver the information they'd gathered on New Taos. Even if Colonel Winter and Dr. Irving couldn't use the city as a new base, he had new data—that crystal from the library. It might be the key to unlocking a new technology they could use.

He had to focus on the bigger picture, the Resistance effort, saving all humans everywhere from the Ch'zar.

He had to let Bobby go.

And if he couldn't get the medicine that Angel needed, he'd have to let her go, too.

It felt like the entire world rested on his shoulders, crushing him. He was only twelve. A few months ago all he cared about was getting good grades and soccer.

Ethan straightened.

The one thing he couldn't afford right then was to feel sorry for himself.

Everyone was counting on him.

"We can't go with you, Bobby," he said. "We have to complete our own mission first."

Bobby's mouth dropped open. He was too stunned to even protest. From his perspective, it had to look like Ethan was abandoning him.

Ethan couldn't even risk telling him what they had to do, because Bobby's mind might become compromised by the Ch'zar, and then the enemy would know everything he did.

"Get the team, Bobby," Ethan said. "Get them and meet me at my house, my old house. That old maple tree in the backyard. I'll be there or leave instructions on how you can find me."

Bobby shook his head, still unable to believe that Ethan wasn't going to help.

Emma stepped in. "Bobby, we have important things to do—things that will save more lives. But we can't tell you the details. . . ." She let her words hang in the air.

"Oh . . . ," Bobby finally said, and a light appeared in his eyes. "Yeah, I get it. Mind control. The aliens would find out, if . . ." He held out his hand for Ethan to shake.

Relief flooded through Ethan. He was glad his old friend understood and wasn't blaming him. That would've been too much to take on top of everything else.

He clasped Bobby's hand and they shook on it.

"I'll rescue them, Ethan. You get your stuff done. Then we'll leave this place together."

Ethan nodded.

Madison handed Bobby her flashlight. "Good luck," she told him.

Bobby gave her a smile. Madison didn't smile back.

Ethan watched Bobby and the other Grizzlies team members go back down the tunnel. He wondered if he'd ever see them again.

It felt like Bobby was taking the last bit of the old, happy, soccer-playing Ethan Blackwood with him.

∘ ∘ ∘ 13 ∘ ∘ ∘

WHAT LIES IN THE DARK?

ETHAN AND MADISON TENSED, THEN SHOVED.

The cast-iron sewer cover grated on asphalt and rasped to one side.

They were crammed in a vertical concrete tube, each with one arm looped through a ladder rung and the other arm on the cover. For Ethan, this was superembarrassing because their shoulders and hips pressed against one another.

He could feel Madison's pulse hammering in her body as they finished sliding the lid off. She was warm. Her muscles were iron cords, but somehow she was soft, too. That had to be a girl thing.

"Are you two going to hang there all night?" Emma whispered. "Are you stuck?"

"We're not stuck," Madison said a little too quickly. She pulled herself up and poked her head over the edge of the sewer hole. "All clear," she whispered back to Ethan.

He clambered after her, and Emma followed.

They stood in the middle of Main Street. Barker's Drugstore was half a block down at the corner. Overhead, those enormous lights held aloft by cranes spilled hard illumination onto the streets and made the three kids' shadows long and spindly.

They ducked into a side street where the light didn't penetrate.

They stripped off their normal-clothes disguises, shoving them into their packs. Their flight suits adapted to their surroundings, turning mottled gray with flecks of red brick for camouflage.

The streets of Santa Blanca looked the same as they always had: smooth asphalt, recently cleaned and washed down by the evening street sweeper; concrete sidewalks; litter cans; and cherry trees in planters every ten paces. All perfect.

Ethan had the strangest feeling, though, that he didn't

know this place. He'd spent his entire life here . . . but Santa Blanca felt empty and dangerous.

"Cut down Elm Street?" Emma asked.

"I was thinking that alley off of Pine," he told her. "That'll dump us out at Tidy Laundry."

"We'll steal a laundry truck," Madison said, "grab some uniforms, and will be halfway out of that Santa Blanca hospital before anyone even notices."

Ethan thought through this improvised plan, listing hundreds of things that could go wrong. Before he got very far, though, he spotted motion on Main Street. A patrol of the Neighborhood Watch adults had rounded the corner. They were swinging their flashlights back and forth into the shadows.

The three Resisters darted down the alleyway.

All it'd take was *one* adult to spot them, and then *all* the adults would know where they were.

They jogged, paused at the end of the alley, checked and double-checked that no one was coming, and sprinted across the road into a narrow side street.

When they were safely back in the dark, Madison said, "There's one thing that's been bugging me . . . about you two."

"Just one thing?" Emma asked, taunting.

"Seriously!" Madison whispered.

It sounded like this was important, so Ethan slowed his pace. "Don't mind my sister," Ethan told Madison. "She's just kidding. Go ahead, what do you want to know?"

"When you woke your I.C.E. suit from hibernation that one day, Ethan . . . ," Madison said, picking her words with great care. "And, Emma, the way you *heard* the Ch'zar mental network back in the tunnel . . . I mean, sometimes I get a whisper in my mind from my dragonfly, but it's nothing like *that*, and I've been training for years to make that strong a connection." She halted. "How can you two *do* stuff like that?"

Ethan heard uncharacteristic fear in Madison's voice. He got the feeling she wasn't taking another step until she got some answers.

"I don't know what it is," Emma admitted. Her usual lightheartedness was gone. "But if you're asking if we're a danger to the mission or the Resistance, if the Ch'zar can read my thoughts as well, then relax. It's not like the two-way communication with our I.C.E.s. With the Ch'zar it's like listening to a radio broadcast. There's no transmission back."

Madison crossed her arms over her chest, and even in the dark, Ethan could sense her skepticism.

Then he did a mental double take.

His sister was *lying*.

When he'd connected on a deep level with his wasp I.C.E. before, it'd almost pulled him under, like he was drowning in a flood of primitive insect thoughts. That's exactly how it'd been when he'd "eavesdropped" on that Ch'zar network back in the tunnel. The tide of thoughts had nearly pulled him in, smothered his personality, and made his mind part of theirs.

The *real* question was how they'd been able to resist the strength of that pull at all.

If he and Emma had the sensitivity to hear it . . . that meant they were somehow *interfacing* with the alien collective hive mind. Their individuality should have been destroyed by that contact.

It was definitely, absolutely *not* passive listening like Emma was telling Madison.

Emma's hand fumbled in the dark and squeezed Ethan's arm.

Was that a warning to keep his big mouth shut? Why?

Ethan remembered how even Dr. Irving had been uncomfortable with his abilities to connect with his I.C.E.—which was mostly Ch'zar-borrowed technology. When pressed, Dr. Irving had cautioned Ethan, *"When it comes to human–insect telepathic connections, we've learned to be cautious."*

Obviously a deep connection where a human mind was controlled had to be avoided at all costs, but what if humans could use the same technology to better control I.C.E.s . . . or even one day use it to influence the Ch'zar?

Ethan shrugged off Emma's hand.

He'd keep quiet about this. He had the feeling it was important, no matter how much it freaked out Madison or the other Resisters. And he got the feeling this had something to do with his parents being able to live in Santa Blanca, to raise him and his sister to be independent, and to do it all without being mentally dominated by the alien collective mind.

"We're okay," Ethan told Madison. "Let's just stay focused on the mission. When we get back to the Seed Bank, we'll sit down with Dr. Irving and he'll figure this all out."

That seemed to mollify Madison, because after a moment, she uncrossed her arms and continued down the alley.

Ethan and Emma followed her and emerged onto Pine Street. Although there was light overhead from the crane lamps, a strange series of narrow shadows zigzagged across the street.

Ethan wasn't comfortable withholding the truth from Madison. He wanted to reassure her that he was still the normal Ethan Blackwood she'd always known, that he and

Emma were still with the Resisters, that there wasn't anything to worry about.

The words, though, evaporated from his lips before he got them out, and the air suddenly seemed to be missing from his lungs.

It was those weird shadows on the street—lines that slanted this way and that.

Ethan could've sworn they tilted to one side . . . and then back. Creaked, even.

Emma froze in place, her mouth wide open.

Something was *very* wrong. The hair on the back of his neck stirred.

Madison elbowed him and pointed straight up.

Ethan's heart stopped as he followed those long shadows to their source.

An ant lion the size of a school bus stood directly over them. Its silver eyes locked onto their comparatively puny forms and its massive jaws opened.

∘ ∘ ∘ 14 ∘ ∘ ∘

MENTAL BLAST

"RUN," ETHAN WHISPERED. "GET OUT OF HERE, you two. I'll distract it."

"No way," Madison whispered back. Her voice was choked with anger that he'd even suggest such a thing.

"That's an order, Corporal," he said.

The ant lion was the larval form of a lacewing. Under natural conditions, this minuscule insect was a formidable warrior that would lie in wait for an ant or similar bug to stumble near a slippery, unstable sand-filled pit it had created. The ant lion would quickly dig the side away, and the doomed insect would slide into the center . . . where the ant lion sat with open jaws.

That was under *normal* conditions—not when the Ch'zar had mutated the creature into a twenty-foot-tall, thirty-ton armored artillery platform with an anti-aircraft cannon mounted on its back and with hydraulically assisted jaws powerful enough to pick up and crush a train car.

The ant lion struck. Its huge jaws slashed down.

Madison rolled to one side. Emma threw herself flat against a brick wall near the alley. Ethan ducked and felt the air whoosh over his head, missing decapitation by inches.

"Sorry," Madison grunted as she rolled to her feet. "I'm a little busy to run away . . . sir." She jumped up and down, waving her arms. "Hey, tin foil!" she screamed. "Over here!"

The Ch'zar ant lion had a silver exoskeleton. It was so reflective that laser beams bounced off it, and the mirror-like quality let it blend in with any environment. It messed with your head, because one second you saw a giant monster in front of you, and the next it practically vanished right before your eyes.

It whirled to face Madison.

"No!" Ethan cried. "Over here! I'm the one you want: *Ethan Blackwood.*"

The ant lion halted as it seemed to consider this.

Ethan gulped. Saying that was *stupid*, but he had to do something to get it away from Madison.

He had the dubious honor of being known to the Ch'zar by name. If an alien collective hive mind could hold a grudge against a single person, it'd be him.

Ethan was the one who'd escaped Santa Blanca, come back and burned the school down, exposed the truth to the kids here, and turned their perfect neighborhood into a police state. He was also the one who'd trashed Sterling Reform School. And Ethan had then led the attack on the command carrier that had been searching for the Seed Bank . . . and possibly killed one of the Ch'zar leaders on board.

The ant lion turned on him—so fast and with such violence that it crashed through Tidy Laundry, crushed walls, and sent plumes of steam into the air. It accidentally brushed Madison aside and sent her flying and sprawling onto the asphalt, dazed.

The artillery mounted on the insect's back ratcheted up and locked into firing position, aimed directly at Ethan.

Yeah, Ethan was definitely on their list.

No time to check on Madison. No time for ducking or dodging.

Ethan flat-out sprinted from the thing.

The ant lion fired its cannon.

The explosion rolled through Ethan. It was a wave of pressure and bone-crunching thunder that left his body feeling like it was filled with mashed potatoes. He was distantly aware that he tumbled through the air, feet over head, hit the ground, and bounced to a stop.

The earth tilted and spun. Blood streamed from his nose. He tasted the stuff filling the back of his throat and spat it out. He couldn't feel his lips. Couldn't feel any part of his body . . . except a pulse-pounding thrum that held the promise of agonizing pain, maybe a broken bone or three, and raw cuts and scrapes through his shredded flight suit.

He ordered his body to stand.

It was like a dream, when you see yourself doing something, not fully in control, just watching it happen.

Ethan got to one knee, planted a boot on the broken road, and then pushed himself to a teetering upright position.

There was smoke, steam, and dust in the air. Shattered bricks lay scattered like a giant jigsaw puzzle. A five-foot-deep crater by the alley where he'd just been standing smoldered with boiling asphalt.

Ethan wanted to lie down and close his eyes, give in to the pulse pounding through his body.

He couldn't.

He had to stay up. He had to distract the enemy long enough for Emma and Madison to escape. He had to fight—no, that was crazy.

There was no fighting a Ch'zar ant lion.

Oh sure, he'd "fought" one before. When he'd been put on the bus to Sterling, Felix and Madison had rescued him outside the Santa Blanca city limits. They'd battled and beaten an ant lion guarding the road. Ethan hadn't really contributed to that fight. He'd stood around while Madison and Felix in their dragonfly and rhinoceros beetle I.C.E.s had engaged in the real combat—and even two against one, it'd been a close call with the Ch'zar mobile artillery.

Here and now, though, Ethan would be trying to fight a living tank with his bare hands.

Not his smartest move.

Through the smoke, Ethan spotted Madison lying facedown, struggling to get to her hands and knees. His first instinct was to go over and help her stand, but that'd only bring the monster closer to them both.

He looked up. There was too much dust and steam in the air to see where the ant lion had gone.

A leg the size of a telephone pole impacted the road next to Ethan. He almost yelped but miraculously kept his mouth shut.

The ant was moving around, searching. Ethan guessed it was confused—it thought it had blown up the tiny crea-ture it had aimed for but couldn't find any trace of it sizzling on the pavement. The dust and smoke and steam weren't making its search easier either.

If it had set that leg down a foot to the left, it would have simply skewered Ethan and ended all its problems.

The ant lion had caused massive damage. The walls of the nearby buildings had toppled over. The streetlight poles lay in the gutters. Electrical lines were down, and a few cables sparked and arced and thrashed on the road like angry snakes.

The adults and Ch'zar really must have had the town locked down not to worry about anyone seeing this.

The ant lion above him shifted once more, and Ethan had to quickly shuffle to one side or get crushed by the great beast's legs.

He had to stay directly under it or risk being spotted.

That situation couldn't last long, though.

The ant lion might see Emma and Madison and go after them. The Ch'zar would be in telepathic communication with this creature, so there had to be enemy backup on the way here. The Neighborhood Watches would get to them first. Maybe they'd even send locust I.C.E.s for air support. The Ch'zar wouldn't take any chances this time on losing Ethan Blackwood.

Ethan didn't think this situation could get much

worse—which was the absolute wrong thing to think, because the instant he thought that, a new wave of pain slammed into his skull.

It was like the blood music he'd heard in the tunnels near those Ch'zar organic conduits, only this was louder, like a hundred people standing next to him and shouting at him.

He shook his head to clear it.

That didn't work, so he clapped his hands over his ears. But that didn't muffle the noise either.

The sound was *inside* his mind.

Was he getting absorbed by the Collective? Or was it some new Ch'zar weapon being directed at him?

Ethan turned, trying to zero in on the origin of the mental blast.

He found it.

Standing in the mouth of the alley, Emma held up one hand toward the ant lion. The great insect took two steps forward, folded its front legs, and bowed down before her.

Ethan's eyes widened. His mouth dropped open.

The source of the noise was *his sister.*

There was only one way so much mental power could be coming from her, only one way a Ch'zar I.C.E. would recognize her as its master.

Emma Blackwood had been absorbed by the Collective.

∘ ∘ ∘ 15 ∘ ∘ ∘

YOU TRY IT

"I'M *NOT* PART OF THE COLLECTIVE," EMMA SAID through clenched teeth. "I'm *using* the Collective to control this thing."

"Using the Collective?" Ethan echoed, not understanding.

Ethan glanced over at Madison to see if she had a clue what Emma meant. She'd only gotten to her hands and knees, though, and still looked dazed from the ant lion swatting her aside.

This had to be a Ch'zar trick to get his trust. There was no way Emma was controlling an ant lion.

But then Emma flashed him a look only his sister

knew—that *why is my brother such a complete idiot?* look.

Ethan wanted to believe she was still in control, still his sister, Emma . . . but he didn't know. If she'd been absorbed, the Ch'zar would know everything she did, including that look.

Emma held up her other hand to stop any more questions. "There's no time," she told him. "There's an ant lion."

"I can see that," Ethan said, exasperated, pointing directly over his head.

"No," she hissed, and pointed past Ethan. "There."

Ethan whirled around. He didn't see anything.

But he did *feel* it.

There was a tremble under his feet. Cracks appeared in the asphalt. Long silver legs the size of telephone poles then stepped over the rubble pile that used to be Tidy Laundry.

It was a *second* ant lion.

"Move out of the way," Emma whispered.

The voices in Ethan's mind turned into screams as Emma held a trembling hand toward the ant lion she had under control.

The insect opened its maw and hissed as loud as a steam whistle. It scrambled toward the other ant lion.

How was she doing that? The noise in Ethan's head

felt like it'd crack his skull. It was like the whisper he got when he connected to his wasp I.C.E., only with the volume cranked up to maximum.

The ant lions clashed. They scrambled to find purchase on one another's bloated bodies, jaws sparking off armor, thrashing legs knocking aside nearby cars as if they were toys.

Ethan pinwheeled back, spotted Madison, and dragged her to the alley.

Madison got to her feet and shoved away Ethan's steadying hands. She took in his bloody face, then glanced at Emma, who had her hands outstretched, mentally directing one ant lion to attack the other.

Madison's gaze locked back on Ethan . . . and her eyes narrowed.

"What is going on?" she demanded.

Ethan heard the accusation in her voice. All things considered, it was hard to blame her. But this wasn't the time or place to explain anything.

The ant lions tumbled into the *Santa Blanca Review* newspaper office and reduced the building to rubble with a tremendous crash. They nearly crushed Madison and Ethan in the process.

Ethan and Madison dodged a landslide of concrete and shattered timbers.

He grabbed his sister's hand as they ran past and dragged her along with them.

Emma stumbled but still kept her other hand outstretched and maintained eye contact with the giant insects.

They got half a block before Madison made a fist and held it up, the signal to halt.

She pointed to the shadows by the side of a building. They ducked into the dark and pressed flat.

Ethan poked his head out and saw a dozen adults in those bright green Neighborhood Watch jackets rounding the corner of Pine Street. They looked normal, like they could've been anyone's parents—if not for the batons they carried and the way they swept their gazes back and forth, heads moving in a synchronized motion, controlled by a single mind.

"We're trapped," Madison whispered. "We can't sneak past those guys." She waved back the way they'd run. "And we'll get squashed if we head that way."

The ant lions stood on their hind legs, wrestling, balanced against one another, jaws snapping, pushing back and forth, turning the entire city block into a disaster zone. Broken fire hydrants sprayed water into the air. Fires erupted from gas pipes. Concrete and asphalt buckled as if they were rumpled cloth.

Ethan snapped his fingers in front of Emma, trying to get her attention.

If only she could make the ant lion run this way. It would scatter those mind-controlled adults, and they could escape.

But Emma ignored him. Her focus on the fighting bugs was absolute.

Ethan looked around and then up.

There was a ledge on the second story of the brick building at their backs. It was Dr. Horatio Ray's medical office. In another life, Ethan had gone there to get vaccines and checkups.

"Madison," he said, "I'm going to give you a boost up to that ledge. See if you can make it to the roof, get a better view, and find a way out of this mess."

Madison looked up, assessing her chances. She chewed her lower lip. Fire reflected in her eyes. "You owe me an explanation, Blackwood," she said.

"You'll get one," he promised her. "But not now."

Ethan meant what he said. He didn't want to keep secrets from Madison—even about his parents. Madison had saved his life more times than he could count. She deserved the truth . . . but more than that, Ethan had to know if she liked him for himself, even the weird parts.

He just couldn't begin to explain it all, not in the middle of a combat zone.

"Okay," Madison said.

She took one last look at the approaching adults and made a motion at Ethan to cup his hands.

He laced his fingers together.

Madison made to step into his offered hands, hesitated, and then leaned forward and kissed his cheek. Her hand touched his face and she lingered.

Her skin was hot. His skin blushed as if she'd set it on fire, burning from the tips of his ears to his toes.

Ethan wanted to pull away, confused . . . and he also wanted it to last for as long as it could.

Madison moved away, though.

She looked somehow happy, worried, and sad all at the same time, and then she stepped into his hands.

Ethan did the only thing he could: gave her a boost up.

Madison grasped the ledge and pulled herself onto it. One last glance down at Ethan and she edged deeper into the shadows.

Ethan touched his cheek.

It was still wet. Her lips had been so soft. Not what he'd expected.

He got a queasy feeling that the kiss was a kiss goodbye.

One of the ant lions screeched with a titanic nails-onblackboard sound as its rear legs lost purchase. It rolled backward, crashing to the ground, and flattened a parked minivan.

Ethan's mind snapped back to reality.

The other giant insect was on its opponent, tearing where the legs met the armored abdomen, snapping and cracking the exoskeleton. The ant lion pulled away and blasted the wounded creature with its artillery.

Ethan flinched at the flash and thunder. The downed ant lion was reduced to chunks of chitin and goo.

Emma collapsed to her knees and cradled her head. "No, no," she whispered. "Ethan . . . *you* have to try."

"What do you mean *I* have to try?"

She pointed at the remaining, living monster ant lion.

As if the creature heard them, its multiple eyes scanned the destroyed city block and spotted them, and then it galloped toward Ethan with amazing speed.

Ethan got it.

The ant lion that'd died was the one Emma had had under her control.

Now they had one living, *very* angry, gigantic ant lion coming to tear them into chunks.

The ground trembled.

So did Ethan.

He tried to gather his courage, but this was way

beyond anything he'd had to face before. He didn't need to be brave to take on this thing—Ethan needed to be *crazy*.

His sister was practically helpless, though. She couldn't run away this time. Madison was safe, but he couldn't count on her staying that way. One stray swipe from that ant lion could destroy the building she'd climbed.

Ethan raised his hand at the charging monster, gritted his teeth, and concentrated for all he was worth.

The ant lion plowed through rubble, snapping power lines and lampposts like they were matchsticks.

Ethan felt the murderous insect mind. It was red-hot, pulsing, and screaming.

But he couldn't get a grasp on it. It was one scream lost in a sea of other screaming voices. Human voices. The voices of a dozen alien races. The Ch'zar Collective.

Ethan mentally recoiled and slammed shut the connection.

He couldn't do it.

The ant lion was close—almost on him and Emma. A hundred feet more and it'd trample them.

Ethan hucked a chunk of asphalt at the thing and jumped to the side of the street.

The insect skidded to a stop and turned on Ethan,

snapping its jaws and hissing. Its breath smelled of gunpowder, blood, and hydraulic fluid.

It was a miracle, but Ethan didn't freeze. Somehow. Either he'd found that courage he needed or he'd gone crazy.

He looked for something to use as a weapon. He almost laughed.

What was he going to use? A stick? A rock?

A bulldozer wouldn't be enough.

His gaze, though, landed on a power line the ant lion had knocked over. The cable sparked and lashed back and forth on the ground like a water hose on full stream.

Ethan didn't think—he leaped, landing right in front of the insect.

He grabbed the power cable. His flight suit gloves were rubberized and insulated against electricity, but not the ten thousand volts pulsing through *this* line. The power made his hands itch and the hair on his arms stand up.

The ant lion was quick, too. As Ethan grabbed the power line, the insect grabbed him.

It scooped Ethan up in its jaws, crushing him around the chest.

Ethan struggled. He couldn't breathe.

The ant lion drew him to its open maw.

Ethan wanted to throw up he was so scared . . . but he didn't. He couldn't. He had only one shot.

The pressure on his chest grew. His ribs flexed and creaked from the stress. The edges of his vision dimmed.

A bit more pressure and Ethan would black out . . . or burst.

The ant lion lifted Ethan up to its inhuman face. A half-dozen silver eyes, each with a tiny black dot of a pupil, tracked him. Its inner jaws opened wide, revealing a million serrated teeth spiraling down its throat.

Worse, Ethan could no longer block the screaming from the insect's mind into his brain.

Ethan screamed back at the thing.

He thrust the electrical cable down the monster's throat.

Ten thousand volts crackled into the ant lion. Lightning arced along its teeth, up its armor, and back to Ethan. Electricity coiled around his flight suit, through the open rips and tears, and made Ethan dance like a shaken rag doll.

All Ethan could see were white stars.

Then nothing *but* white.

Then nothing.

∘ ∘ ∘ 16 ∘ ∘ ∘

CAMOUFLAGED

ETHAN'S FIRST THOUGHT WAS THAT THE ENTIRE Grizzlies soccer team had just played a championship bout on his chest wearing their half-ton cybernetic suits.

It hurt to even take a breath.

He breathed anyway, shuddering in lungfuls of air.

At least he was alive.

He thought.

If you were dead, could you feel this bad?

He flashed back to the ant lion lifting him up to its tooth-lined maw. Adrenaline jolted through his body. His eyes popped wide open and he tried to sit up.

Restraints on his wrists snapped taut. His waist, thighs, and ankles were strapped down, too.

His thoughts took a moment to readjust. He was no longer about to be devoured by a monster. That was good.

He was no longer electrocuting himself either. That was good, too.

But he didn't know where he was. . . . He wasn't even sure he was still in Santa Blanca.

He recognized what this place was, though: a hospital room.

Ethan lay on a gurney on a white pad, heated from underneath for comfort.

That was it in the coziness department, though. The restraints on his wrists were unpadded, a quarter inch of leather chained to the rails of his bed. An IV had been set up, and an orange fluid dripped through a needle puncturing his inner arm. Whatever it was, it burned inside and made him feel definitely weird, like his head was full of cotton candy.

The place smelled of rubbing alcohol. The overhead lights were dim, and the only real illumination came from the biomonitors that beeped in time with his heartbeat.

Ethan tugged once more on his restraints. His wrists had a half inch of play, and then nothing. There was no way he'd muscle his way out of this situation.

Someone was breathing next to him. He turned and saw a girl wearing a surgical mask step from the shadows.

She removed the mask. It was Emma.

She put her finger to her lips, indicating he must keep his mouth shut.

That was hard, considering he had a *zillion* questions—and considering that in Emma's other hand was a syringe filled with some glowing silver liquid.

She stepped toward him, brandishing the needle.

Ethan squirmed in place.

It was like when Coach Norman had tried to drug him. He'd told Ethan they would put him in a coma, then chemically cause puberty so they could absorb his mind once and for all.

Emma was one of them now. She was the enemy.

"Oh please," Emma whispered, and rolled her eyes. "Why don't you just assume the *worst* possible thing in the entire world that can happen?" She plunged the needle into the plastic tubing of the IV drip.

The silver fluid from the syringe reacted with the orange stuff in the IV solution, spreading into the reservoir and down into his arm. It was freezing cold and felt like it was worming through his biceps, across his chest, and up the side of his neck.

Whatever it was, though, it cleared his head.

"What is that stuff?"

Emma examined the empty syringe and shook her head. "Don't know its name." She turned it and showed him an octagonal symbol on the side. Within the shape was a complicated series of dots and lines.

It looked like some of the indicators in his I.C.E. cockpit.

If Ethan had to guess, he'd say it was a Ch'zar symbol.

"I know what it does, though," Emma said, squinting and swiping her thumb over the symbol. "It neutralizes the chemical cocktail they've pumped into you. One that would have accelerated the puberty process."

She patted his arm and gave him a smug smile. "Don't worry, little brother. You're still a year behind me. Plenty of time to grow up."

Ethan bristled at this—as if he hadn't already grown up enough to lead an entire squadron into battle while she'd still been clueless about the real world.

Emma cocked an eyebrow. "Although from that kiss Madison planted on you . . . you might be further along than I thought."

Ethan blushed. That kiss hadn't been *his* idea. And it wasn't what Emma thought it was.

Was it?

"Get me out of here," he said.

He still wasn't convinced this wasn't some Ch'zar trick.

Of course, they didn't *need* a trick. They could just force him to undergo puberty. Ethan would then be one of them, and they'd know everything he did.

Or would they?

Maybe, like Angel had said, he was different. Maybe there was a part of his brain the Ch'zar could never reach. Like his parents, living in a Santa Blanca neighborhood right under the collective noses of the Ch'zar.

"I'm keeping you tied up for a minute," Emma said. Her expression sobered and she straightened her braid. "I need to explain a few things before you go off and do something 'heroic' and bring everyone in this place running after us."

Ethan lay back. He let out a huge exhale. "Fine."

This was *so* like his sister. Sometimes when she had a midterm, instead of studying all night like everyone else, Emma would take a big break and eat chocolate chip cookies, waiting until the very last moment to go through her stack of three-by-five cards to memorize facts and formulas.

She said her brain worked better under pressure.

Sounded crazy to Ethan, but it was hard to argue with her straight-A average.

"Just tell me one thing," Ethan said. "If you're *not* part of the Collective, why would they leave you here unrestrained with me? The Ch'zar are a lot of things, but they're not dumb."

"No . . ." Emma's gaze drifted away. "They're not. They're actually smarter than any of us thought."

This statement didn't fill Ethan with confidence.

Her eyes snapped back to him. "That's beside the point. Look, I need to tell this my own way. Stop being a lieutenant in the Resistance for a minute, drop the 'rather die than give an inch' attitude, and just be my brother."

He made a pathetic gesture of surrender with his bound hands.

"I never stopped being your brother, Emma. Go ahead. I'm listening."

She took a deep breath. "Okay. This started a while ago, when I was a little younger than you are now. I heard whispers at home. Voices in my head." She snorted a laugh. "Well, I wasn't crazy enough to tell anyone I thought I might be crazy. I thought it was just the strain of studying and getting ready for high school entrance examinations. Those voices, though, went away when I was near Mom or Dad."

Emma pressed her lips together and stopped.

Ethan knew how she felt. He could *think* about his parents, but to *talk* about them . . . *that* was tough.

"When the Ch'zar took me and you burned down the school," she continued, "those voices were about the *only* thing I could hear. They *almost* talked me into joining them."

She closed her eyes.

"And when they stuck me in Ward Zero at Sterling, I heard the other kids when they got absorbed into the Collective. I could still hear their voices, but then they got drowned out by a larger choir of voices around them. They lost their individuality, I guess."

Emma opened her eyes, but they were unfocused, as if she were looking into the past.

"That's when I learned *I* had a voice, too," she whispered. "I could sing. I could join in the chorus . . . without actually getting *lost* in it."

The blood music. That's what she had to be talking about. Ethan held his breath. He'd heard it in the tunnels and when the ant lion had screamed directly into his mind. He shuddered.

"It was hard at first," she said, "but after you rescued me, when I started interfacing with my ladybug I.C.E., she taught me new songs, and it got easier."

Ethan frowned. He'd never heard "music" from his wasp. All he ever sensed was that pulse-pounding drum-roll of hunger and the urge to kill. Maybe that was a kind of primitive music; he wasn't sure. Or maybe everyone heard the mental connection a little differently.

"I'm singing right now," Emma said. "Just a little off-key. Just enough to disappear as an individual to the Collective's mental 'ear'—but not enough so I become one of them. To them, though, it sounds like I'm *guarding* you. They won't come if they think you're being watched by one of them."

"Wait," Ethan said. "You're telling me that you're blocking the *entire* Collective from your mind?"

"That would be impossible," Emma said, and crinkled her nose. "There are too many. And they're too strong. Sometimes I can give one person in the Collective a mental nudge, make them blink or look the other way for a second, but nothing major. What I do is more like camouflage. I think that's what Mom and Dad did for years while they were living here."

Ethan shook his head. "*I* can't do that."

"You can't do it *yet*. You're such a child sometimes, Ethan. You're a lot stronger than you think."

She unbuckled the restraints on his wrists.

"Which brings us back to your first question: Why

would the Ch'zar leave me with you? They didn't. Mental camouflage is one thing. But I had to wait until they'd drugged you and left you alone, *and* I had to wear this."

She pulled out the surgical mask she'd been wearing before and twirled it around her little finger.

"If anyone saw my face, it'd be a disaster. They'd be sure to recognize Emma Blackwood, on the Ch'zar's most-wanted list after escaping from Ward Zero with her notorious brother."

Emma cast a nervous glance at the door, and then once more covered her face with the surgical mask.

She leaned over to undo the restraints, and Ethan could've sworn he heard her singing, although her mouth wasn't moving. She had to be humming.

"We've got to be supercareful," she said. "I can pass as one of them with this mask on, but all it takes is for *one* of them to spot us and they'll *all* know."

"So," Ethan said, sitting up and rubbing his wrists, "if you have all these new mind powers, does that mean you've gone through puberty already?"

"That's *none* of your business, Mister Ethan Black-wood!"

She helped him get to his feet and slugged him in the shoulder.

"Ow!"

It wasn't so much that the punch hurt him (it did), but his body turned from the force and his chest felt like his ribs had been pounded with a sledgehammer.

"Come on, Emma. Answer the question," he told her, rubbing his side. "It's a fair one. It's nothing personal. It matters to everyone."

Now it was Emma's turn to fidget.

She grabbed her braid and twisted it, and then finally said, "No puberty. Not yet."

Growing up in Santa Blanca, they'd been taught about puberty and the changes that happen to your body. Outside of biology class, though, it was considered in poor taste to talk about the subject. It could even land you in detention.

Ethan saw that this had been a smoke screen used by the Ch'zar to keep information about puberty—who was going through it and, more importantly, how everyone who hit puberty got "graduated" to high school—a huge secret.

At the Seed Bank, this was turned completely on its head. *Everyone* talked about it. You even had a doctor take blood samples every week to test hormone levels. Results were posted outside the mess hall. It was *all* out in the open.

None of that, though, made it any easier for Ethan or Emma. They had a lifetime of brainwashing to shake off.

If Emma hadn't hit puberty yet, what would happen when she did if she was in close contact with the Ch'zar Collective *now*?

Ethan had to make sure his sister was isolated *before* puberty. It could be a total disaster.

A stab of panic then plunged into his heart. "What happened to Madison?"

Emma held up both hands to calm him down.

"She got away," she said. "I've picked up whispers from the Collective—they're looking for all the Resisters in town. So far, they haven't found any of them."

Ethan nodded. That was *one* piece of good luck . . . but it wouldn't last forever.

He examined himself. Someone had dressed him in a hospital gown. There were bandages underneath—and no flight suit! He felt naked. He practically *was* naked! The only thing besides bandages covering him under the flimsy cotton were ugly black-and-yellow bruises.

"Still in one piece?" Emma asked.

"Yeah," he said, and coughed. "More or less."

"Good," she said. "Because it's time to do your hero thing, little brother . . . or should I say, *Lieutenant* Blackwood."

Ethan took a good long look at Emma, trying to decide if he believed her or not. Was she still his sister? He rubbed his shoulder. The Ch'zar probably wouldn't have punched him like that.

"Okay," he said. "Just tell me, where the heck are we?"

"In a Ch'zar facility, under Santa Blanca," she said. "There are miles of corridors, laboratories, and machine shops, and a hundred people I never saw before."

Ethan looked around the tiny hospital room for anything they could use.

One of his high-risk escape plans began to take shape in his mind . . . one he *really* didn't like.

○ ○ ○ 17 ○ ○ ○

THEY KNOW!

EMMA WHEELED ETHAN OUT OF THE HOSPITAL
room on his gurney.

They'd quickly ransacked the place before they left
but hadn't found anything labeled (in human words or
Ch'zar icons) as antiradiation medicine. Angel was cooked
if they failed to find something to help her.

Ethan squirmed on the gurney, uncomfortable and
anxious in the half-buckled restraints that Emma had re-
attached around his wrists and the surgical mask half
smothering his face.

"Lie still," she told him. "You're supposed to be
knocked out from the drugs."

Ethan couldn't help it: he *had* to peek through his nearly closed eyes.

The gurney trundled down a corridor lined with blue tiles, past tiny rooms filled with other kids. They were crammed in, two to a bed, hooked up to IVs, and sleeping . . . or more accurately, they'd been drugged into comas.

These had to be the "sick" Santa Blanca kids Bobby had told him about. They were supposed to have been shipped out to the hospital in Haven Heart, but apparently, unknown to any of the kids left behind, that hospital was a prison located right under the town.

The Ch'zar had taken the kids who had seen I.C.E. suits battle, kids who had suspected there was something strange going on with their parents, kids who were learning the truth, and removed them from the population. They were accelerating the puberty process and would absorb their minds.

Ethan felt sick.

He wasn't doing this to them. It wasn't *his* fault.

In a way, though, it was.

If he'd never come back to rescue Emma and burned down the school, none of this would be happening now.

No. He couldn't think that way.

These kids would get absorbed no matter what. If not now, then in a few years.

Ethan wanted to jump up, rip out their IVs, and help them all escape.

He might've tried, too, if the place hadn't been full of adults.

Grown-ups crowded the corridors. They wore hospital lab coats. They all seemed to have to be somewhere in a big hurry. No one spoke a word. They tracked him and Emma as they wheeled past, as if they suspected there was something "off" with them, but they didn't stop them.

Ethan realized that he was holding his breath.

He very slowly exhaled through the mask.

One big gasp would've let everyone know that Ethan Blackwood, supposed-to-be-comatose Ethan Blackwood, was very much awake.

And if they were caught now, Ethan and Emma would be sedated, and he knew this time he wouldn't wake up.

Emma shoved the gurney onto an elevator. Three adults crammed in with them.

Ethan froze. All they had to do was take a careful look at him to see that he was sweating—something a person in a coma *wouldn't* be doing either.

He couldn't help it.

And to top it off, Ethan now had to go to the bathroom.

Despite all that, he kept one of his eyes slightly open.

The elevator was glass, and as they rose, he saw a huge cavern beyond.

Within the great open space, giant industrial robots with multiple arms moved cargo containers, stacking them like toy blocks. There were rows of I.C.E. locusts on a runway. Their wings buzzed experimentally, and to Ethan it looked as if they were itching to take off and get into battle. Crawling along the cave's walls were black ants the size of cars.

This place was a hive, and it looked like it was waking up, getting ready for something.

But what? The Ch'zar had the "information leak" in Santa Blanca more or less under control. They weren't gearing up to destroy an entire city just because Bobby and a few of his Grizzlies teammates were on the loose.

Ethan had read in school how army ants would move out in a huge swarm and destroy *everything* in their path.

He steeled himself, suppressing the shudder he felt coming.

Before he unleashed a colossal shiver, the elevator pinged. Emma must've sensed Ethan was about to blow it, because she rammed the gurney through, just as the elevator doors started to close. They left the three adults behind.

"No one's here," Emma whispered.

"How do you know?"

"I can feel them in my head . . . stronger when they're closer."

Ethan shivered finally—head to toe.

"There." Emma pointed down a tunnel that wormed into the shadows. Its walls were rough, and the occasional bare lightbulb revealed a dirt floor. "It leads back to the sewers, and out."

Ethan shucked off his loose restraints, jumped off the gurney, and started down the corridor.

"But," Emma said behind him, "you're not going to like it."

Ethan didn't stop. Whatever was down there couldn't be worse than the hospital, all those mind-control doctors and the kids about to lose themselves.

He was so wrong.

The tunnel spilled into another enormous cavern, this one with stalactites and stalagmites that looked like they were poised to snap shut.

Ethan halted, his mouth open. He exhaled a tiny squeak.

Lined up in rows, some piled together in heaps, others disassembled and laid out like a jigsaw puzzle, were I.C.E. units—black and red ants, locusts, orange-and-white rhinoceros beetles, honeybees, dozens of mosquitoes, half a centipede, and even a circus-tent-sized wing of a monarch butterfly.

None of these bugs twitched a single antenna. In fact, most of them—all of them, Ethan saw—were partially taken apart.

There were wound spools of silk thread, riveted sections of ceramic exoskeleton, tangles of hydraulic lines, blinking LED indicators, pistons, jet engine fan blades that looked like metal daisies, radar dishes, segmented eyes, machine guns, and ruby-tipped lasers.

It was so quiet that Ethan only heard his heart pounding.

He wondered what had happened to the few Ch'zar I.C.E.s that had had human pilots. Had they been saved?

"Repair bay?" Emma whispered, stepping closer to his side.

"More like a graveyard," Ethan whispered back.

Along the far wall, his gaze landed on titanic limbs that looked like the pointed fingers of a fairy-tale giant. In the weird bioluminescent half-light cast by the glow-worms creeping along the ground, he saw that the limbs glimmered silver gray.

It was one of those terrible ant lions.

No . . . not *an* ant lion . . . *the* ant lion.

The monster's maw was wide open, spirals of teeth

exposed, scarred and charred with jagged carbonized lines that Ethan had etched with a sparking electrical cable.

In a trance, Ethan moved toward the beast he'd slain.

He felt as if he just *had* to see the thing again.

In any other circumstances, he would've run away, but he couldn't feel anything living from its mind. Just a few hours ago it had screamed directly into Ethan's brain. Now the lack of any mental activity was so thick about it that it seemed like a hole in space instead of a solid object.

Ethan crept within five feet of the ant lion. Its abdomen armor plate had been hinged open, and the heart and stomach organs (part tissue, part metal, and part plastic) had been removed and set upon the floor. A bundle of optical cables had been dragged out from the inside, too, and hooked up to a black twelve-sided shape about a foot across. This device was covered with the strange Ch'zar dot-and-dash icons.

Emma reached out. "There are thoughts," she said, "moving. It's like they're being transferred from the ant lion and stored in that thing."

Ethan stopped.

Thoughts? Why would the Ch'zar need to transfer those? They were all mentally linked, unless the electrical damage had somehow fried part of the insect's brain.

In a flash, Ethan got an idea.

He had a feeling this might be superdangerous but also superimportant.

"This is our chance to *spy* on them," he told Emma. "And do it without a deep dive into their Collective mind. We have a piece of what they know *right here!*"

Emma and Ethan looked around the cavern to see if there was any movement, but there was nothing.

They stepped closer to the broken I.C.E.

Emma reached out. Her left hand hovered over the black device. The icons lit with pink- and blue-ice-colored lights. Emma inhaled sharply and with her right hand grasped Ethan's hand.

The mental link was sudden and sharp.

Ethan sensed everything Emma was sensing, streaming from that black box and the connection to the ant lion's damaged nerve bundle.

There came flashes of emotion so primitive no words could describe them. They were more violent than the murderous thoughts Ethan had picked up from his wasp. It was more brutality than he could imagine.

Sensations burst through. First, smells: the plastic odor of hydraulic fluid; the sugary, salty tang of the slime in the reserve fuel tanks; blood, smoke, and ozone.

Next came sounds: a fragment of the Ch'zar hive mind song . . . so many voices and not all of them human.

Ethan recoiled, but Emma held his hand firmly, and his mind snapped back to the connection.

And last came visions: hatching from a giant egg and climbing out with uncertain legs; taking wobbly steps on the sandy floor of the nursery cave; eating and fighting and clambering over the hundreds of other juvenile ant lions; firing artillery with thunderous reports at a diving wasp I.C.E. as it swooped down, snatched a train car, and smashed it into a mountainside (that had been Ethan at the Geo Transit Tunnel!); scrabbling through a forest, knocking over trees, and digging through smoldering wreckage.

Ethan recognized this last scene as showing the remains of the Ch'zar command zeppelin that Sterling Squadron and the other Resister pilots had destroyed. The Ch'zar had come *so* close to finding the Seed Bank.

Then the image of a distant mountainside that Ethan had never seen before. The ant lion had so fully camouflaged itself in the surrounding rocks and foliage that it couldn't even see its own limbs. There was motion on the mountain, and then a stream of wasps and hornets emerged from a hidden tunnel.

The Ch'zar didn't use that hornet breed. Those were Resister I.C.E.s.

Ethan pulled away from Emma.

She broke contact, too, and turned, astonished, to Ethan.

"That was Jack Figgin's squadron," Emma whispered. "The Black and Blue Hawks."

"I know," Ethan told her. "The Ch'zar have seen the Seed Bank entrance." He felt the blood drain from his face. "They know where our base is."

18

MEDICINE

ETHAN AND EMMA BOTH STOOD THERE, STUNNED.

Ethan's head spun. The Seed Bank's location was the *one* secret the Ch'zar were never supposed to find out . . . because if they did, they could destroy the last fortress of free humanity.

He glanced at his sister. She twisted the end of her braid into a knot of worry.

"They couldn't know," she whispered. "They would've attacked already."

"I wouldn't," Ethan said slowly. "Not after the pasting we gave them the last time they got close. I'd wait, regroup, and be one hundred percent sure that I had enough force to make the next battle totally lopsided."

There was a moment of silence between them.

Ethan couldn't believe this, even though he'd "seen" it himself. It was his worst nightmare.

"Do you think that's why they're here? In these caverns?" Emma asked. "So many enemy I.C.E.s"—her eyes unfocused—"lying in wait, hidden under the neighborhoods?"

Ethan could see it in his mind, laid out as if it were a map. If he were the Ch'zar, he'd gradually build up his forces in secret and ring the Seed Bank. Then he'd spring, not giving an enemy that had beaten and outsmarted him so many times before *any* chance to escape the trap.

"We have to warn Colonel Winter and Dr. Irving," he said.

"Is there time?" Emma asked with a tremble in her voice.

"There has to be."

He started toward the far tunnel, the one that Emma had told him led to the sewers and outside, but then halted.

"Wait," he said. "There's one more thing. This is a repair bay, right?"

"Sure," Emma said, "but we've got to—"

"And since," Ethan said, cutting her off, "like our I.C.E.s, the Ch'zar I.C.E.s are part mechanical and part *biological*, that means they might have some—"

"Medicine," Emma finished for him.

"Maybe something that can help Angel," Ethan said.

They hadn't found any medicine for radiation poisoning in Ethan's hospital room. Why should they have? Santa Blanca kids normally didn't come in contact with radiation (rare leaks from their nuclear-powered athletic suits aside). But Ch'zar I.C.E.s had microfusion reactors and flew through restricted regions all the time. *They* had to have a way to deal with radiation.

Ethan and Emma searched a rack of equipment near the ant lion. Ethan found arc welders, air-impact wrenches, and hydraulic fluid tanks. Nothing that would help.

"Over here," Emma said. "A first-aid kit, I think."

He went to her and a large chest she'd opened.

It was full of those flat living bandages the Resistance used to make field repairs on their I.C.E.s. Smaller versions had been used on himself, Felix, and other wounded pilots.

He poked one of the caterpillar-like creatures. It squirmed.

One tiny box had a strange dash-and-dot Ch'zar icon. It looked like jumbled Morse code. Ethan ran a finger over it. The icon's meaning snapped into focus in his thoughts.

"That's the alien symbol for radiation, isn't it?"

Ethan didn't know how he knew that. It worried him.

Emma's eyes narrowed at the icon, and she nodded.

Ethan slipped the latch on the box and opened it. Inside was a syringe. The sight of the needle made him pull back. So many times people had tried to poke him with needles—it kind of freaked him out.

Next to the syringe were six clear vials. Within them was a liquid that glowed an intense lime green . . . a color similar to the toxic radiation warnings on their flight maps.

"Radiation," Emma said. "Does that mean it's a cure for it, or that it *is* radiation?"

Ethan touched one of the vials. It was warm.

The icon on this box lacked any context. Emma was right: it could be a cure for the radiation, or it could *be* radioactive.

"What it is is a chance for Angel," he whispered. "Unless we take a risk and try this, she has *no* chance at all."

Emma pressed her lips into a single white line of concern.

Ethan snapped shut the box and scooped it up. He

tried to adjust the flimsy hospital gown he'd been put in but failed to feel any more covered.

"So what now, Lieutenant?" Emma asked. "Do we stick to the plan and find Felix and the others and get back to the Seed Bank?"

Ethan hesitated. Ultimately all of this was his responsibility—their mission, their lives, now even the fate of the Seed Bank and the last free-willed humans in the universe.

Things had been so easy a few months ago, when all he had to worry about was how to win his next soccer game and how to pass the occasional pre-algebra quiz.

He was Lieutenant Blackwood, though, not just a soccer player or pilot. He felt confident *and* terrified, all at the same time.

"We'll stick to the plan," he finally told Emma. "But there's one place I want to go back to first, a place I have a feeling we'll never get another chance to see unless we go now."

He looked at her.

Emma's face contorted with confusion, then smoothed, and one eyebrow shot up.

"Home," he told her.

19

NOT YOUR HOME ANYMORE

ETHAN AND EMMA SNUCK THROUGH THE STREETS
of Santa Blanca. He felt ridiculous still wearing the hospital gown. It was very . . . breezy. There was no time to search through backyards to find laundry drying on lines.

There was really no time left to go back to their old house either.

But Ethan felt that he *had* to go back, just one more time, to see the place where he and his sister had grown up. They had to go there because Ethan had the weirdest feeling that he'd missed *something* when he'd searched his house in a rush.

Whatever it was, it called to Ethan, pulled at him like a magnetic force.

His parents?

Franklin and Melinda Blackwood wouldn't come back here, not if any part of their selves remained. They'd only be back in Santa Blanca if the Ch'zar had gotten to them.

Ethan shivered. This hospital gown barely covered his body. The streetlights on cranes were dark. A low fog clung to the streets and oozed over the neighborhood lawns.

Flashlights stabbed through the misty darkness ahead.

Ethan pulled Emma up a driveway. They crouched behind trash cans.

A pack of a dozen adults walked down the sidewalk past their hiding spot. This was not a Neighborhood Watch, because there were kids with them, still dressed in their pajamas, some almost as old Emma, but some so young their parents had to carry them. The kids murmured complaints. None of the adults spoke.

Emma started to whisper a question, but Ethan held a finger to his lips and pointed down the street.

More groups of adults and kids crossed at the intersection. They moved to where the school used to be.

Something was going on.

Maybe the Ch'zar had already figured out they were missing from the underground hospital. That wouldn't rate a full-scale evacuation from Santa Blanca, though. Were Bobby and the other Grizzlies causing trouble? Were Felix and the rest of Sterling Squadron doing something? If they'd gotten the I.C.E.s cleaned and operational, there could be a full-scale battle raging in the city right now.

Ethan strained to hear anything—the whisper of giant wings in the sky, the clash of exoskeleton armor, a distant explosion.

But there was nothing. Not even the crickets were awake at this hour.

Whatever the Ch'zar were up to tonight was making the hair on the back of Ethan's neck stir.

He signaled to Emma and they moved out.

They were like ghosts in the neighborhood where Ethan and Emma had played hide-and-seek, sold lemonade on the corner, gone trick-or-treating, shot off those great model rockets, and had the time of their lives.

Ethan would have given anything to feel that untroubled again.

They rounded the street corner, and he halted to draw in a deep breath.

A Victorian house stood in the dark. Its wide wraparound porch beckoned to them like open arms. Even at night, Ethan could still make out the friendly gingerbread trim.

The Blackwood residence.

His heart sank, though, as he spied the mailbox. It read THE HANSENS.

Of course, someone else had to be living here now. The Ch'zar wouldn't waste a perfectly good house.

Emma and Ethan circled around back. Through the window on the back porch, he saw the light over the oven was dark. His mom had always kept it on. It felt wrong to see it unlit.

Ethan eased open the back door—there were no locks on any Santa Blanca house—and they slipped inside. He felt like a thief in his own house.

But this wasn't his house anymore, was it? The Hansen family lived here. Probably a gaggle of kids and parents who were part of the Collective . . . which meant they were dangerous.

"I don't think anyone's here," Emma whispered. "It feels empty."

Ethan felt it, too. Not a creak. Not a breath from another human in the entire house.

They snuck upstairs and checked every room.

The beds were unmade. Clothes had been tossed onto the floor. It looked like everyone had left in a big hurry.

The Hansens might have been one of those groups they'd seen on the street.

"What are we looking for?" Emma asked.

Ethan shook his head. "I don't know . . . something."

He wandered into his room. There were posters of van Gogh sunflowers on the wall. The homework on the desk had the name *Jane Hansen* scrawled across the pages.

Ethan felt strange that the room he'd grown up in was now a girl's room.

His eyes widened. "Mr. Bubbles!"

His betta was on the windowsill. The blue fish was asleep.

Ethan tapped the bowl and Mr. Bubbles twitched, woke up, and swam to the top, looking for food.

He'd completely forgotten about his pet. He was so glad someone was taking care of him.

Ethan sprinkled food for Mr. Bubbles. "There you go, guy."

Emma crossed her arms. "We came here to feed your fish?" She looked around his room, snorted, and strode out.

Ethan tapped the side of Mr. Bubbles' bowl, sighed, and then reluctantly left him. Jane Hansen was taking better care of him than he could.

Emma went to their parents' old room.

"You said there's a secret compartment in Mom and Dad's closet?" Emma opened the closet door, searched, but found nothing.

"This side," Ethan told her. He pushed on the closet wall. It felt solid. "There has to be a catch."

Emma pulled Ethan out of the closet. She took two steps back, then turned around and planted a martial arts kick smack on the wall. The Sheetrock caved in, leaving a hole the size of a dinner plate.

"Don't!" Ethan said. "You're going to get us in trouble."

Emma's eyebrows quirked and she gave him a look that said, *my poor stupid brain-damaged brother.*

"Seriously?" she asked. "You're worried about a busted wall after you burned down the school, crushed the Geo Transit train, and blew up a hundred other things?"

Ethan frowned.

He pulled at the edges of the hole Emma had made in the wall.

Within was the safe he'd seen before. It wasn't locked and opened with a tug.

There was nothing inside.

"The Ch'zar must have cleaned it out," Emma muttered. She exhaled a huge sigh. "Come on. There's nothing for us to find here."

Ethan couldn't believe it. He'd been so sure there'd be another note, or some *super*secret hidden compartment.

He double-checked, smoothing his hand along the inside of the safe.

There was a single half sheet of paper in the dust.

He pulled it out, his heart racing.

Emma moved closer. Standing on tiptoes, she peered over his shoulder.

Together they read it:

~~31,~~ May

We wish we could explain. If you've come back to save ~~Emma and the twins,~~ though, you must know part of the truth.

~~And~~ you know why we cannot explain.

We have ~~the twins.~~ We'll be safe.

It is our wish ~~one~~ day that ~~there will be zero trouble~~ we'll all be reunited under the open sky. Then ~~the two of us~~ we will explain everything.

All our love, ~~Two big hugs~~
Mom and Dad

Ethan's heart sank.

"It's a first draft of the letters they wrote us," Emma whispered, the disappointment thick in her voice.

He squinted at the page, turning it over and over. There was nothing on the back. It was basically the same letter his parents had written to them—just with a bunch of words crossed out. Nothing more.

Tears pricked his eyes. He missed Mom and Dad so much. He wished this had been instructions, an explanation, a note telling him where they were now, something . . . but it was only confirmation that he and Emma were on their own.

"I don't get it," Ethan said. "Mom and Dad had so much of this planned." He riffled the note. "Why leave *this* in the safe? Why not tear it up so the Ch'zar wouldn't find it? Or just burn it?"

"Maybe they were in a big hurry," his sister replied.

Ethan's mom measured out every ingredient, put them in bowls, and lined them up alphabetically before she started baking cookies. His dad had every tool labeled and up on Peg-Boards, sorted by function, inside the shed.

They *didn't* just leave scraps of paper around for their enemies to find.

A tremor shook the house and rattled the windows.

Ethan and Emma rushed to the bedroom window.

A huge shape moved in the shadow of the maple tree in their backyard.

Ethan caught a flash of gold in the starlight and inhaled sharply.

It was a wasp.

His wasp!

∘ ∘ ∘ 20 ∘ ∘ ∘

WHAT ETHAN LEFT BEHIND

"THAT HAS TO BE STERLING SQUADRON DOWN there," Ethan told Emma. "Let's go."

Emma grabbed the note from his hands. She gazed at the page as if it were the most precious thing in the world. She smoothed and folded it and then tucked it into her flight suit.

Ethan wanted to tell her not to bother, that it would be best to forget their parents and their past and the lies they used to live in Santa Blanca. They had work to do. Part of him, though, was glad she had the courage to keep the note. It was the last bit of their parents left.

They ran downstairs and burst out the back door.

Ethan felt his wasp before he got a good look at it. That connection with the beast's mind snapped into place. It was fueled and clean and ready for action. Hungry.

The wasp crouched under the maple tree. Its black and gold stripes seemed to ripple, making it hard to see in the moon shadows. Its stinger laser, though, gave it away as it smoldered in anticipation of combat.

The abdomen armor section hinged open with a hiss, inviting Ethan into the cockpit.

Tremors shook the ground as a huge rhinoceros beetle landed in the backyard. Emma's ladybug joined it, flattening a rose hedge, and in rapid succession, more bugs crunched the fences and toppled over trees and sheds in the neighbors' yard. Paul's praying mantis, Angel's wasp, Kristov's locust, Oliver's cockroach, Lee's housefly, and Madison's whisper-quiet dragonfly lit upon the roof of the house.

Sterling Squadron.

Ethan had never been so happy to see a swarm of bloodthirsty bugs!

Madison climbed out of her dragonfly and dropped to ground level off the roof. She covered her mouth as she saw Ethan in the hospital gown, but then saluted. She turned and scanned the surrounding neighborhood, looking for threats.

Ethan's face burned with embarrassment. He tried to close the back of the open gown. How ridiculous.

He wished there was time to talk to Madison alone. Ethan wanted to explain more about what was going on with his and Emma's minds. He wanted to ask what in the world she had meant by that kiss back on Pine Street, too.

Felix's beetle seemed to melt into the blue-black shadows. The cockpit opened and the sergeant eased out and strode toward Ethan. There was a giant smile on his face. He looked like he was about to hug Ethan, but stopped and smartly saluted.

Ethan felt as if he was going to die in front of his squad in that half-open hospital gown. He saluted back.

"Report," Ethan said.

"Squadron I.C.E.s are cleaned and scrubbed, Lieutenant," Felix said. "No trouble . . . except a dozen crashed cars, one totaled trash truck, and Laurel Street is flooded from burst fire hydrants. No injuries. We set the autopilots in your wasp, Emma's ladybug, and Angel's wasp to 'follow-me mode.'"

"Fill me in on the details later," Ethan said. "I'm just glad to be back in business. How's Angel?"

The smile on Felix's face faded. "Worse. She has a high fever that we can't bring down."

"We have something that might help," Ethan told him. "Where is she?"

Felix waved at the mantis and the black wasp. Paul's ghostly green I.C.E. opened, and he dropped out, then dragged Angel from her cockpit. Paul looped one of her arms around his neck and marched her closer. Felix and Paul eased the unconscious Angel onto the lawn.

She was pale and covered in sweat. The neck of her flight suit had been torn and scratched as if she'd tried to claw the thing off.

Ethan knelt and felt her forehead. She was burning up. It was the kind of fever they should bring her to the hospital for (except the nearest hospital was actually an alien-controlled prison).

Emma knelt by them, too. She produced the small box they'd liberated from the Ch'zar repair bay. In a businesslike manner, she opened it. The glowing vials inside illuminated her grim face.

"What's that?" Felix asked, studying Emma's features.

She didn't answer. She attached a vial to the syringe, cleared the instrument of air bubbles, and without hesitation plunged the needle into Angel's neck.

Angel, even semi-comatose, gasped in pain.

"It's medicine," Emma explained. She didn't meet Felix's gaze.

After a second, Angel's breathing slowed and deepened.

Ethan decided not to clarify that this was Ch'zar medicine . . . at least, *Emma* thought it might be medicine. Okay, it was fifty-fifty that this was either medicine or *more* radiation. But what choice was there?

Ethan also chose not to mention that he and Emma could sort of read Ch'zar icons. Just like Emma could hear the Collective's song in her brain.

There was no time to get into those things now, not when one fact took priority over everything else—even Angel's life.

"The Seed Bank," Ethan whispered. "We found out something."

Emma felt Angel's forehead. "Wait. She's getting hotter." She took one of Angel's hands.

Paul, surprisingly, took Angel's other hand.

Angel groaned and started to thrash on the lawn. Emma held her as best she could, and then Angel stopped moving altogether.

"Is she . . ."

Ethan tried to say, "Is she okay?" but he was thinking, *Is she dead?* What if they'd made a terrible mistake by injecting her with that stuff?

Seconds ticked away.

"Her fever's breaking," Emma finally said. "She's

breathing normally. Pulse is high but dropping to close to normal."

Ethan exhaled, relieved that the medicine *might* be working. He didn't especially like Angel. She was trouble, but she was also part of the squad and, he had to admit, a natural combat pilot.

Paul's face was tight with worry, making the scar on his cheek all the more visible. He relaxed a tiny bit. "Good work, Blackwood," he said.

There was something new in Paul's voice, something personal, like Angel was more than just a wingmate to him. It was a surprise to see Paul care about someone other than himself for once.

"The Seed Bank. You were about to say something about it?" Felix asked.

"There's no easy way to tell you guys this," Ethan said. "Emma and I think the Ch'zar know where it is."

Felix stared blankly at Ethan, too shocked to say anything.

"That can't be," Paul said. "They'd have wiped it out."

"Not necessarily," Felix whispered, and looked over his shoulder. "It might explain why we've seen massive civilian movement and no I.C.E. activity in the area."

"A buildup?" Paul said, his eyes glazing over.

"A sudden preemptive strike," Felix replied.

"Get Angel into her wasp," Ethan ordered. "We're flying out. Now that the I.C.E.s are cleaned, we have a chance to avoid Ch'zar detection. Our priority is to get back to Colonel Winter and report."

At the mention of his mother, Felix turned pale in the moonlight. "Yes, sir," he said, and helped Paul carry Angel back to her wasp.

Emma stood, closed the box of Ch'zar antiradiation treatment, and went to Ethan's wasp. The side cargo panel opened at her approach.

How had she ordered his I.C.E. to do that? It annoyed Ethan that *she* was giving *his* wasp orders.

She rummaged inside, pulled out a spare flight suit, and marched back to Ethan.

"Here you go, Lieutenant," she said, thrusting the suit into his arms. "There should only be *one* full moon out tonight."

Ethan awkwardly tried to cover his back in the hospital gown. Failed.

He flushed again, this time from his toes to the tips of his ears, and then gave up trying to be modest and stepped into the high-g combat flight suit. The self-fitting pressure cuffs cinched tight around his ankles, hips, chest, and wrists.

A perfect fit. He felt like a Resister pilot once more instead of an escaped mental patient.

"Wait, Felix," he said, jogging over to Angel's black wasp I.C.E. "I don't understand how you knew that Emma and I would be at our old house."

Felix positioned Angel in her cockpit. She seemed to be sleeping peacefully now. Paul patted her cheek and sealed her inside.

"Oh, that," Felix said. He pointed to the corner of the backyard. "Them."

There were a dozen kids in the shadows. Bobby stepped forth, his lips set in a grim straight line.

Ethan smiled and went to him. "You guys made it," he said, and extended his hand to shake.

Bobby looked at Ethan's extended hand but didn't take it.

"We got here," he whispered, "just like you told us to, Ethan. Picked up a few along the way." He nodded over his shoulder.

Some of the kids behind Bobby were members of the Grizzlies soccer team. But some Ethan didn't recognize. They had torn clothes, bloody knuckles, and one had a broken arm in a sling.

"It was pretty rough," Bobby said. He shook his head and his dark curly hair fell over his eyes. "We lost a few."

Ethan set a hand on his friend's shoulder. He knew

what it was like. He also knew that nothing he could say would make Bobby feel any better.

"We found your team," Bobby continued. "We helped them get those things"—he gestured at the I.C.E.s—"cleaned up. I told them you said to meet here."

Ethan was glad to see Bobby alive, but he had a growing feeling of unease.

He remembered how he and Bobby had parted in the tunnels. He'd told Bobby to meet him in his backyard by the old maple tree.

Bobby had said he'd rescue as many kids getting shipped out by the Ch'zar as he could . . . and told Ethan they'd all get out *together*.

Ethan withdrew his hand from Bobby's shoulder.

That last part had been entirely Bobby's idea.

Ethan hadn't had the heart to say it at the time, but he hadn't thought Bobby would be coming back.

"You can't come with us," Ethan whispered.

Bobby's head snapped up. "What do you mean? That was the plan. We can't make it out of here on our own. You've got to help us!"

"Our cockpits are too small. There's room for just one person," Ethan told him. It killed Ethan to admit that, but it was the truth.

"I don't care!" Bobby shouted. "Just carry us, then."

"We've got to get back to our base," Ethan continued. "There's going to be trouble on the way. Probably combat. You guys would be in too much danger."

Bobby laughed. "And how much danger do you think we'll be in if we stay here?"

"I don't know. I only know that I have a mission to finish. Once I do that, I'll come back and—"

"Save your breath," Bobby said. "I don't believe you. Once you're gone, we'll never see you again, you coward."

He turned his back on Ethan.

Ethan stepped toward him.

Bobby spun around and socked Ethan on the chin.

A month ago, a strike like that would've knocked Ethan over. Now Ethan just took the punch, and his head snapped to one side. With a busted lip, he stood his ground and stared back at his former teammate and friend.

Felix and Paul took a step closer, hands forming into fists, ready to pound Bobby.

Ethan held up a hand, warning them to stay back.

"Make for the tunnels," he told Bobby. "The Ch'zar are moving out. They won't look for you there. Keep one person posted by your house. We'll try and meet you there *if* we're alive at the end of the day."

The rage drained from Bobby's face as it dawned on him that *he* really wasn't the only one in trouble.

Ethan turned and left him there. He felt like a traitor. Like a murderer.

He also knew he was doing the only thing he could.

A month ago, he would have gathered the Santa Blanca refugees in a bus and carried it off with I.C.E.s.

A big metal bus, though, would light up Ch'zar radar. They'd have a fight on their hands. Not only would that compromise his mission but also it'd very likely get the civilians killed.

His duty to the Resistance was more important.

If he was right that the Ch'zar knew about the Seed Bank, Sterling Squadron would have to fly fast and low and probably still fight through enemy lines to get back to the base.

He clambered into his wasp's cockpit.

This was the problem that Ethan had been wrestling with since Colonel Winter had made him Lieutenant Blackwood and put him charge. All too often, there was more than one right choice. He could only pick one. He had people counting on him to save their lives, and he couldn't save them all.

Authority. Responsibility. Accountability.

He hadn't wanted any of it . . . but those things were his now.

He closed the hatch.

"Mount up," Ethan said via the short-range radio. "Let's move out."

With a rumble of thunder, the squadron lifted into the air.

Ethan looked down. He didn't see Bobby or the others. They'd already disappeared into the shadows.

"Good luck, guys," he whispered, and with a sigh added, "I'm so sorry."

JAMMED

EVERYTHING WAS DIFFERENT.

It wasn't just leaving Bobby and the other Santa Blanca kids behind, although that was part of it. Ethan could never go back to being the Ethan Blackwood who just played soccer and did his homework. That old life seemed like someone else's.

But it was more than that.

Being in his wasp's cockpit *felt* different.

The configuration was the same. Surrounding him were arrays of hexagonal displays showing the aft, fore, port, and starboard views of the night sky and the terrain below. There were radar images of the squadron around him, thermal readouts, radio logs, and a dozen other I.C.E. systems. There were winking, blinking indicators, icons, and the steady breathing of air vents.

The *different* part was that Ethan now understood the icons. Oh, he knew what most were from his training. He'd been told and had to memorize the weird dot-and-dash symbols for the ejection controls, autopilot, and laser-coolant warning systems, and a million other things . . . but the real difference now was that he could *read* them.

Some of the systems his trainers had never shown him were "pollen extractors," "venom reserves," and something that best translated as "molecular density overdrive."

It all sounded neat, but Ethan wondered if Resister technicians had never told him about these things because it was an aspect of the Ch'zar I.C.E. system *they* didn't know.

Another difference was a feeling that he belonged here. Like he'd been born to be part of this wasp. For a moment that twisted into a smothering sensation—Ethan felt for a second like he was drowning—and it was all he could do to not scream and claw his way out of the suddenly claustrophobic cockpit.

The wasp's mind clicked into place, though, completely under *his* control.

The feeling passed.

It was like they were flying together, not just pilot and I.C.E. but a single creature. Ethan felt wind rushing over his skin at four hundred miles an hour.

This had to be a side effect of all the weird stuff he and Emma had been experiencing in their brains—hearing the Ch'zar Collective song, even hearing the static in his mind back at New Taos (probably the mind of the city's controlling computer network). It was like his brain was learning to link to things, not just to his I.C.E. suit.

Would it eventually pull him in? Make him such a deep part of the suit that he lost Ethan Blackwood? Like all those kids they'd put in the enemy I.C.E. suits at Sterling Reform School?

He shuddered and felt the connection to his wasp ease off.

Ethan exhaled and tried not to freak out. The new, stronger mental connection seemed voluntary . . . for now.

He had to stop thinking about himself. He had his squadron to worry about—and they might not all be alive much longer if the Ch'zar were really preparing a major strike against the Resistance.

He tapped the wide-focus control under his left hand.

Images of the I.C.E.s in Sterling Squadron flashed on the screens around him in their relative flight formation.

Each insect's data poured onto the screens in a jumble of animated bars, indicators, and wriggling Ch'zar icons.

Dead ahead on the smallest screen was Madison's dragonfly. Its sleek form was outlined by his computers; otherwise she would've been invisible against the stars. All the dragonfly's running lights were off and her jet exhausts baffled to obscure her infrared heat signature. She had pulled ahead of the group—zipping along in a serpentine flight path at just under the speed of sound.

Ethan caught a flicker of emerald green as she arced up to thirty thousand feet to get a better look at the airspace.

On his wasp's immediate starboard side was Emma's ladybug. He counted five black dots on the insect's armor. In the moonlight, the ladybug was the color of blood, reminding Ethan that while her I.C.E. was "cute," it was an assault-scout hybrid and a match for any unit in the squadron.

He could've sworn Emma was looking back at him, and for some strange reason, he got the idea she wanted to punch him in the shoulder like she always did. Maybe if they both weren't flying several tons of bug at half the speed of sound, he'd have been comforted by that "ordinary" gesture.

To his immediate port side was Paul's ghostly green praying mantis. Its forelimbs were extended as if it were about to pounce on some imaginary prey.

Ethan saw that Paul's hydraulics were slightly over-pressurized, causing the limb extension. He thought about warning Paul, but he might be running it that way for an extra burst of strength in combat. Risky, but Ethan decided not to meddle with his pilots' preferences.

On Paul's port side was Angel's black wasp, looking like the shadow to his I.C.E. Indicators showed it still ran on autopilot, but Ethan thought he saw the unit sway back and forth, almost playfully.

Felix was aft in the formation, the "anchor" position. His gigantic midnight-blue rhinoceros beetle was a dark moon in the sky. Readouts indicated the unit was fully loaded with bombs, and his particle-beam capacitors were at full charge. There was enough firepower in the bug to take on an entire army.

Kristov held their formation's point one hundred feet ahead of Ethan. The red locust was a blur of wings and spiked legs and looked ready to tear the next bug it came across limb from limb.

Every indicator on the locust's status was in the green. It was impressive, considering that only four weeks before,

Kristov had been just another bully at the Sterling Reform School and never been in the air.

Oliver's cockroach was fifty feet under the main formation, the "ventral" position. His I.C.E.'s exoskeleton glistened, reflecting the stars.

Lee's housefly drifted over and around, not settling in any particular position in the formation. His I.C.E. was small and fast and almost impossible to get a weapon's lock on.

The squadron's equipment was combat ready, but what about the pilots?

Shortly after they'd taken off, Ethan had briefed them about the Ch'zar knowing the location of the Seed Bank. He told them they might be in for the battle of their lives. To their credit, they didn't say a word. They just formed up around him and flew like professionals.

Ethan opened up the short-range channel. "Squadron report."

"All systems ready," Felix said with steely confidence in his voice.

"Good to go," Emma chimed in.

"Yo," Paul added with a practiced boredom that Ethan had come to understand was his way of dealing with stress.

"Ready here," Kristov replied.

"I'm all set," Oliver said, and nervously cleared his throat.

"Me too," Lee added, although it sounded like he might throw up at any moment.

Angel's radio link was open, but she was silent. Her autopilot indicator was still lit.

Madison hadn't checked in.

"Corporal?" Ethan asked. "Situation report."

Madison's voice came over the radio, but it was choppy and awash with static. Ethan strained to hear but couldn't make out a single word.

She was ten miles ahead and now at thirty-five thousand feet. Maybe there was interference at the higher altitude. They were at the limit of the short-range radio, but he should have heard *something* coherent.

Ethan had a bad feeling about it.

He considered opening a longer-range radio channel. They needed to stay hidden, though, so Ethan signaled the squadron to accelerate and climb another thousand feet to close the gap.

Madison's voice broke through the static: "—ionic charge up here jamming our signals. Like a thunderstorm, but there are no clouds, so it's got to be artificial."

Ethan's bad feeling turned into a ball of ice in his stomach.

Tonight wasn't the night to believe in coincidences and weird out-of-the-blue weather effects.

"Close up, Madison," he said.

The dragonfly cooled its jets and drifted back into formation.

"I'm not picking up a signal from base," Madison said. "It's not the normal blackout procedure either. It's the same thing that happened near New Taos. The frequencies are being blanketed with broadcast static."

That had to be the Ch'zar.

"Everyone slow to one-sixty and go to winged flight," Ethan ordered.

The roar of jets around him cut out and the I.C.E.s went to wing power.

Ethan wanted time to think and check his maps.

He connected to the satellite feed and overlaid it on his cockpit displays. They were approaching the Cumberland River Valley in the Appalachian Mountains. Five minutes until Security Protocol 003 kicked in and their visuals blacked out. The satellite view flashed over elevation lines, rivers, and distant neighborhoods.

If the Ch'zar had some big invasion planned, Ethan would've spotted something in the air by now.

But nothing showed up on the map.

Usually there was *something*—a robotic cargo carrier, a single army ant on patrol, even distant fireflies flitting on overwatch around a Ch'zar factory.

Everything was completely quiet tonight.

He calculated a flight path between the zones covered by the Ch'zar "eyes" in low orbit.

Maybe he and Emma had overreacted when they'd seen that image of Resister I.C.E.s exiting the Seed Bank in the ant lion's memory. Couldn't the enemy just have written it off as a rogue Resister flying out of some cave? What evidence that the Ch'zar had discovered the Resisters' base of operation was one picture?

The hairs on the back of Ethan's neck prickled, though.

He closed his eyes and tried to imagine what was ahead.

Not a whisper . . . not a trace of the Ch'zar Collective song. Whatever "mental" airwaves were out there, they were silent tonight.

Ethan exhaled.

Okay, he was getting paranoid.

"Go ground flight," Ethan commanded. Protocol demanded that they come in to the Seed Bank low and fast if they could before the cockpit blackout occurred. That minimized any chance of being spotted by the enemy.

Sterling Squadron tightened formation and dove.

If Ethan could get to Colonel Winter with this new warning and the information they'd found in New Taos, the senior officers would come up with a plan to stop the Ch'zar or find a new base.

Then Ethan could go back and rescue Bobby and the others in Santa Blanca.

Everything might turn out okay.

The squadron approached the summit of the Blue Ridge Mountains. Ethan saw pine treetops below and a river glistening in the moonlight. They crested the ridge of a mountain and zoomed back down the other slope. And Ethan's heart stopped beating at what he saw.

A mountain valley spread out before him a dozen miles wide, and on the far side was another set of mountains, blue granite, covered in snow . . . and Ch'zar.

On the ground, a solid mass of black army ants marched, a quarter-mile square of interlinked insects, tearing up the forests and meadows and overturning every rock in their path as they spread across the valley.

Half-mile-long centipedes slinked among the destroyed terrain, leaving trampled trails in their wake.

Ant lion artillery squatted on the surrounding hills. Normally camouflaged, they lit up Ethan's infrared imagers as they blasted shells into the air. Artillery arced up and impacted the mountainside, blasting free house-sized chunks of rock.

In the air, four command carriers—like the one that had tried to find the Resister base before—floated like gigantic storm clouds. Each zeppelin combat platform was surrounded by dozens of squadrons: locusts, bumblebees, and mosquitoes.

To Ethan's dread, he saw that the nose of each carrier bristled with spikes and angled panels. Those were defenses, so he couldn't repeat the trick of blasting through the aircraft and blowing it up from the inside out.

Static crackled over the radio, and only then did Ethan pick up combat chatter from Jack Figgin's Black and Blue Hawks, Becka's Bombers, and every other Resister fighter squadron as they engaged with the enemy.

The Ch'zar had somehow jammed their radio signals—even jammed their Collective song from Ethan's mind. They were learning new tricks faster and faster.

It dawned on Ethan that this would be the last battle for the Seed Bank.

It would be the last battle for the Resisters.

° ° ° 22 ° ° °

COUNTERATTACK

ADRENALINE SURGED THROUGH ETHAN AND HIS wasp. His jets roared to life, and the stinger laser flared with heat.

His first instinct was to rocket forward and fight . . . but they were on the wrong end of this battle.

That was a good *and* a bad thing.

It was good because the Ch'zar were formed up to attack the mountain. Ethan could catch them off guard and hit their backside.

It was bad because he'd only get in one good attack and then be enveloped without the support of the other

Resister squadrons in the air, who were on the far side of the combat.

And there were a *lot* of enemy units between them.

Ethan counted five, maybe six, squadrons of enemy I.C.E.s, and *more* poured out of the launch bays of the combat carriers. As he watched, a full dozen squadrons formed up in the air—green locusts, red-and-black wasps, clouds of mosquitoes, even a superfast swarm of orange dragonflies. For every Resister squadron near the mountain—Becka's Bombers, Jack Figgin's crew, and the Flying Pirates—*three* enemy squadrons broke and attacked them.

Meanwhile, army ants spread out and made a ring around the mountain base. They tore at the rock, sparks showering up as their superstrong mandibles pulverized the stone.

Ant lions continued to shell the mountainside. Sheets of rock avalanched down, revealing steel plates underneath.

This wasn't just any mountain. It was the Seed Bank under there!

Ethan was seeing the Resister base for the very first time. Of course, if it *was* the base, why hadn't being so close triggered Security Protocol 003? Their viewscreens should've been blacked out by now.

Colonel Winter had to have turned off the security protocols so the Resister pilots could fight.

The four Ch'zar command carriers tilted up and rapidly rose above the battle, lining up in a row pointed at the mountain. They were going to try something.

Ethan had to try something, too.

Before one of Ethan's crazy plans could form in his head, though, a squadron of titanium honeybees peeled off and sped toward them. Each enemy bee was heavily armored, and instead of pollen baskets on their hind legs, they sported missile racks.

Two dozen of the tiny missiles whooshed at Ethan and his people. The bees hit their afterburners and followed them in toward Sterling Squadron.

"Counterattack formation delta!" Ethan cried over the radio. "Go!"

Sterling Squadron scattered to shake off the incoming micromissiles. Those missiles would never have a chance to lock on, and when Sterling's I.C.E.s circled back to engage the bees, the Ch'zar would have to self-destruct the missiles or risk getting blasted by their own weapons.

Ethan dove and used his wings to helicopter around one hundred eighty degrees, then hit his jets. Three missiles streaked past his forward viewscreen, unable to bank tight enough to follow his maneuver.

His wasp met the lead titanium bee, latched on, and tore its head off.

Three more bees immediately grabbed on to him.

Ethan was ready for that old trick. He had his stinger laser primed, and he aimed and flashed one at point-blank, leaving a gaping hole in the creature's chest.

As the remaining two tried to chew off his wasp's wings, Ethan angled his jets at them, opened the throttle, and blasted their titanium faces, washing the stunned insects off his back.

Around Ethan was the chaos of massive aerial combat.

Missiles streaked and left crisscrossing trails of exhaust. Rocket-propelled grenades thumped and detonated on exoskeleton armor, shattering both enemy and Resister I.C.E. shells. Laser and particle beams lit up the night as if it were the Summer Fireworks Festival back in Santa Blanca. Punctuating the fire and flashes, artillery shells looked like exploding supernovas and left smoky, smudged dots in the air.

Paul's green mantis darted before Ethan, holding twitching locust limbs in either of its front claws.

Emma became a whirling machine of death, firing bombs in every direction, turning enemy I.C.E.s near her into smoldering bits of wreckage.

Felix's rhinoceros beetle used its heavy particle beam

to spray destruction in a wide swath and melted off the wings of six incoming Ch'zar beetles. Their plummeting wreckage continued to glow red-hot until it hit the ground and exploded, taking out hundreds of wriggling, screaming army ants.

Through the smoke and fire, Ethan made out Jack Figgin's squadron as they engaged a dozen squadrons of enemy locusts over the mountain.

Seed Bank exit tunnels collapsed inward, leaving rubble-filled craters—no more friendly I.C.E.s would be getting out of the base.

Jack's Black and Blue Hawks tore through the enemy, flashing lasers, firing missiles, and going claw to claw. Locust bodies dropped from the air, but they kept launching from the carriers, and Jack's people were getting boxed in.

"Jack!" Ethan shouted. "You're surrounded. Circle around. Link up with us. We can—"

The signal from Jack's I.C.E. went dead.

Ethan spotted a fireball where he'd been a moment ago.

Ethan stared, stunned, as more Resister I.C.E.s were taken out. A handful broke free from the firefight and jetted into the cloud layer above the battle.

"Watch out, you idiot!"

A black bug crashed into Ethan, knocking his wasp into a barrel roll.

Ethan shook off the shock of Jack's death and the skull-rattling blow he'd just taken, and spun, laser ready . . . to see Angel's black wasp grappling with two titanium bees, both of which had every missile still in their hind-leg racks, primed to detonate.

Firing missiles hadn't worked, so the Ch'zar were going to make sure this time they took out at least *one* Resister I.C.E.

Angel was awake, though. She was fighting.

She'd saved his life while he'd been hovering in the middle of a battle like a complete fool.

Ethan fired his laser, slicing off the hind legs of one of the bees latched on to her wasp. It was a precise shot that severed the limbs at the joint, missing the stack of missiles by inches.

The bee's legs tumbled away and detonated with enough power to pulverize the wasp I.C.E. had it been attached.

Emma came out of nowhere and crashed into the remaining titanium bee, effortlessly peeling it off the black wasp and tossing it aside—but too late. The Ch'zar bug exploded ten feet from her. The black-spotted ladybug

I.C.E. tumbled end over end through the air, legs twitching, wings motionless.

Ethan rocketed after his sister.

He caught the ladybug and stopped its free fall, but he had to use his jets on full power. Emma's bug was *so* heavy.

As they slowed, Ethan saw a spiderweb of stress cracks shoot over the ladybug's outer shell.

Worse . . . he couldn't feel Emma's mind inside her I.C.E. anymore.

His palms turned clammy. His heart skipped a beat.

"Emma!" he shouted with his mind. "Wake up!"

If his sister was dead because of his stupidity, he didn't know what he'd do.

The ladybug suddenly grappled with him and, annoyed, shoved him off.

She was back, the song of her mind strong in his thoughts and mostly broadcasting embarrassment at having to be rescued by her "little" brother.

"I'm okay," Emma said on the radio, struggling to regain her breath.

"Blackwood!" Another girl's voice broke over the radio.

It took him a second to recognize it. "Rebecca," he replied.

He switched to the encrypted commanders' frequency. "Where are you? How can we help?"

"Glad you made it home, Ethan," Rebecca said. "We could use a hand over here." Her words were casual, but her voice crackled with tension. "We're doing a run on the lead Ch'zar carrier. If we can take it out, that might start a chain reaction and take them *all* out."

Ethan told his wasp to watch out for incoming enemy units, and then he turned his attention to the line of ascending enemy carriers.

He saw Rebecca's plan in his mind. If her bumblebee bombers could hit the first zeppelin and *if* they could blow it up, they could set the whole line of enemy carriers off like a string of firecrackers.

Those were some big ifs, though.

The last time he'd faced a Ch'zar command carrier, Ethan had risked killing his best friend and sister to blow it up. But now the Ch'zar had compensated for the carrier's one known weakness by covering the nose with spikes and deflecting armor plates.

Without a vulnerable spot to hit, there was no way for Becka's Bombers to even get close. Covering the top of the zeppelins were platoons of defending ant lion artillery—able to blast anything that flew overhead into dust.

"What do you know that I don't?" Ethan asked.

"Some physics," Rebecca said with smugness. "A little

underhand toss so we don't get cooked by their topside defenses."

It was so simple Ethan should've thought of it. Becka's Bombers were more than bombers. They were insects with flexible joints and superstrength. They didn't have to *drop* their bombs. With a flick of their bodies, they could lob them *up* to the carriers.

They'd still have to get awfully close, though.

So that's where Sterling came in.

"We'll have you covered," Ethan told Rebecca. "No matter what it takes."

"I was hoping you'd say that," she said.

He switched frequencies back to his squad.

"Sterling, mop up the local enemy forces and then get back into formation. We're going in."

∘ ∘ ∘ 23 ∘ ∘ ∘

PILLAR OF FLAME

STERLING SQUADRON MOVED AWAY FROM THE mountain battlegrounds and climbed to twenty thousand feet. Becka's bumblebee bombers were going to join them up there, but the heavy bomber units were slower to climb.

Ethan couldn't help but watch the carnage unfold below as army ants tunneled into the mountainside and artillery pounded the slopes. A quarter of the solid rock mountaintop had been sheared off. How much more pounding could the Resisters inside take?

Every second that ticked away was one less second the Seed Bank had left.

His throat tightened as he thought about Dr. Irving, his mentor, the scientist who had seen Earth invaded by the Ch'zar and the military strategist "storm falcon" who had survived the previous world war. He was Madison's grandfather, too. Ethan had to make sure Dr. Irving was safe. He was too important to the Resistance, and too important to Ethan, to have any harm come to him.

He set those feelings aside. They weren't helping up here.

Ethan did a quick systems check of the Sterling I.C.E.s.

All green—although Emma's and Kristov's units had an overall yellow flight rating with leaking hydraulics and compromised exoskeletons.

It'd have to be good enough.

He reviewed Rebecca's proposed flight plan. First, a parabolic dive to gain speed. If her numbers were right, they'd skim the ground only a dozen feet over the rocks.

Second, they'd pull up at maximum velocity and appear directly under where the first Ch'zar carrier would be a minute from now.

Third, her bombers would release their payload underneath the carrier, with a flick of their bodies for that last extra push. The bombs' momentum would carry them the rest of the way to their target.

Fourth, the Resister I.C.E.s would scatter . . . and hope.

They'd have to get lucky to crack the heavy armor on the underside of the carrier, to have it catch fire and then explode and set the other nearby carriers on fire, too.

It was a wild, crazy plan, a plan that Ethan might have come up with himself. That didn't stop his fears from bubbling up inside him, though.

Rebecca and her bumblebees finished their climb and hovered alongside Sterling Squadron. The bees were a matte black and golden yellow. Their undersides were sky blue and white. There were only ten left in her squadron, and many leaked oil or had legs missing. Each, though, gripped a half-ton bomb that was composed of high explosives, fuel, and ceramic carbide shrapnel spikes designed to penetrate armor.

It just *had* to be enough firepower to take down one of the Ch'zar command carriers.

"Are we good, Blackwood?" Rebecca asked on the private commander channel.

Ethan wanted to add something to her plan. Wasn't that what lieutenants were supposed to do?

He stopped himself, though. Rebecca had been making bombing runs for years. She knew the capabilities of her equipment and people far better than he did.

In other words, he should let Becka's Bombers do their part, and Sterling would do theirs. He was realizing that was part of command, too: knowing to keep your mouth shut when you couldn't add to the solution.

"It's a solid plan," he told her. "Sterling has you covered."

He looked to either side and saw his people arranged in a wedge. Felix and Emma flanked him, Madison and Oliver were directly behind, Paul and Kristov were on his starboard wing, and Angel and Lee were on his port wing.

Ethan had point on this one.

Their mission was to clear a path and take on all enemies that could interfere with the bombers' run.

"Follow me in," Ethan told Sterling Squadron.

He dove, leading the way. Ethan let the wasp fly on the preprogrammed route. He focused on firing his stinger laser, blasting a score of escort mosquitoes that darted in from the port side.

Emma and Felix poured on the heat with their particle beams, and together they left a trail of melted mosquito shrapnel in their wake.

At the bottom of their dive, a full squadron of locusts leaped into the air and intercepted them. Ethan fired and caught the lead enemy bug between its open jaws. It tumbled off course and crashed into a cluster of army ants on the ground, squashing six of them.

Felix and Emma kept firing, clearing the way. Paul

grabbed on to a locust that got through their particle beams and tore it apart. Lee's housefly flashed quick laser bursts and blinded another, and sent it groping and crashing into a bank of hillside ant lion artillery.

Trees, rocks, and the snaking form of a huge centipede filled Ethan's screens as Sterling Squadron pulled up from the dive.

He felt his skin and muscles strain against crushing acceleration. The g-forces were too much to take. The edges of his vision danced with black stars.

Fortunately his wasp was tougher and held the flight path, not easing up until they were almost vertical.

The pressure then subsided a little and Ethan's senses came back to him.

Overhead was the huge underbelly of the Ch'zar command carrier. It looked like the biggest thunderhead cloud he'd ever seen. Bristling from its side were cannons, missile ports, and I.C.E. launch bays.

A swarm of yellow jackets poured from the enemy zeppelin.

Ethan lasered the lead fighter and it crashed into its wingmate. Emma and Felix launched bomblets and shattered the shells of the next half dozen.

Bug parts rained onto the battlefield below. The way was clear for Becka's Bombers.

Ethan glanced at his aft camera. He counted nine bumblebees rising through the smoke.

They'd lost one.

He gritted his teeth and wished he could have saved that person. He'd done his best, though. He just hoped it was enough.

"Scatter," he ordered Sterling. "Pattern omega."

His wasp veered to starboard and rolled, dodging a stream of automatic gunfire from the lower curve of the carrier as anti-aircraft guns popped out.

Ethan switched his aft camera to the central display.

The bumblebees rose to the apex of their climb in a disorganized pack. Some flared their wings to slow, while others lit afterburners, and the group tightened into a single wall of I.C.E.s that perfectly mirrored the shape of the carrier's underside.

Ethan marveled at the precision flying.

The bees opened the claws that clamped the bombs. Each bomb was the size of a car and strangely floated alongside the bees for a split second—then the I.C.E.s flicked their bodies and propelled their payloads up, at the same time giving themselves a big push away from the carrier.

The bombs flew in a perfect dotted line.

They hit.

Nine lightning-bright flashes went off together, blossoming into white flowers of death, expanding into boiling clouds of burning fuel that dulled to amber and then hellish red, enveloping the carrier from underneath.

A shock wave rippled up through the superstructure. It bent the frame, ripped the skin, and undulated to the top, where it shattered the outer shell and sent the ant lion artillery stationed there flying.

Meanwhile, the undercarriage caught fire. Flames licked at the sides and sent tendrils of oily smoke curling into the air.

They'd done it!

Swarms of enemy I.C.E.s dropped from the undamaged carriers and rushed to their sister ship. They sprayed foam down the sides. The substance stopped the fire from spreading higher, but it evaporated and couldn't dribble down to the flames underneath.

At the aft end of the burning carrier, a huge valve dilated open and expelled a whoosh of gas.

The carrier immediately sank toward the ground, using its huge tail fin to steer toward the forest and a stream below.

It pulled up at the last moment, skidding and crashing through the trees and plowing through the river.

Water and earth smothered the flames. Before it could reignite, enemy I.C.E.s were on the craft, spraying it down with fire-suppressant foam. Clouds of steam and smoke billowed into the air.

That was smart. The Ch'zar had saved one of their command carriers . . . but it was definitely out of the fight. Good.

Ethan's happiness vanished, though, when he turned his attention to the *rest* of the Ch'zar fleet.

The remaining three command carriers were surrounded by clouds of defending I.C.E.s. There'd be no way to make another bombing run—even if they had more bombs.

The initial bombing run had been textbook perfect, but the Ch'zar had put out the fire before the first carrier had exploded and there was no chance now to stop those other carriers.

The Ch'zar had learned so many new tactics since they'd last engaged the Resisters.

And that was Ethan's doing. He'd fooled them too many times and taught them to be tricky . . . just like him.

The three Ch'zar command carriers continued their slow approach toward the mountain and the Seed Bank.

Ethan's mind raced through the possibilities. Should he try to launch Emma and Felix again, maybe *all of them*, at the nose of the carriers and hope they could blast through the new defenses? That seemed like the only way to take them out. Or was he missing something obvious? Some *new* way to trick the Ch'zar and win?

He *had* to figure out something.

They'd made him a lieutenant, put him in charge—it was *his* responsibility.

"Blackwood." Colonel Winter's voice broke through on a private radio channel. She sounded in control and irritated, like the enemy finding the Seed Bank and blowing it off the map was a minor inconvenience that she'd get fixed in a second.

"Ma'am, I think I could stop—"

"There's no more time for plans," Colonel Winter told him. "I have new orders for you. These will be my last, so listen carefully for once."

"Colonel," Ethan said, and tried to figure out how to tell her there *was* a way to win. Sure, a stupid and likely-to-get-them-killed way, but hadn't he always found a way to survive his crazy schemes?

Before his thoughts could form into words, though, Colonel Winter continued. "You are to evacuate," she said. "Take Sterling and hide."

"I don't understand, ma'am."

"Run, Blackwood. Far away. As fast as you can go. Once the enemy is done here, they're going to hunt you personally, I think."

Ethan couldn't believe he was hearing this from the colonel. She never gave up.

"I'm sending similar orders to Rebecca to go, but *not* with you. This will maximize your chances for survival." Colonel Winter's voice, usually full of steel and authority, wavered. "Tell Felix," she whispered, "tell him I love him . . . that I wish I could have shown it more. Tell him he is to carry out Special Order Eighty-Eight. And tell him . . . his father would've been proud of him, too."

The cockpit swam around Ethan. He couldn't believe this was happening.

It had to be some new Ch'zar ploy. They were using the colonel's voice to trick him.

"I won't run, ma'am," Ethan told her. "I can't leave you and Dr. Irving behind."

"I understand," she said, shocking Ethan that she wasn't yelling at him. "In a few moments, though, there's going to be nothing left behind for you to save. You have your orders, Lieutenant. I know you'll find a way to make it. The Resistance will live on through you."

She took a deep breath and when she spoke next, all the steel had returned to her voice: "This is Colonel Amanda Winter, signing off."

The radio channel went dead.

Ethan stared at the speaker, stunned.

"Ethan!" Felix shouted through the speaker, snapping Ethan out of his daze. "The Ch'zar are approaching the Seed Bank. What are your orders?"

Ethan couldn't give up. He had to fight.

But he had the most horrible feeling about what the colonel had just said: *"In a few moments, though, there's going to be nothing left behind for you to save."*

Ethan knew under no circumstances would she let the Ch'zar capture them. With her and the other adult Resisters' minds added to the Collective, the enemy would know every secret and weakness of the Resistance. And if that happened, Sterling Squadron, her son Felix, none of them would have a chance.

He decided.

Orders and responsibility had their place. That wasn't now.

"Line up on me," Ethan told the squadron. "We're making another combat run at those carriers."

"Wait," Emma whispered. "You've seen the carriers' new defenses. I don't think we can make it this time. And with all those I.C.E.s defending, I don't think we'll even get close."

"Just do it—or don't!" he shouted at his sister. "We've got to help." Tears blurred his vision and he rapidly blinked them away. "We've got to . . ."

The words faded from his lips as the lead Ch'zar command carrier rose a thousand feet over the mountain. Along its belly, doors parted. Hundreds of bombs tumbled out, each looking like a spiked seedpod, each the size of a house.

The bombs hit the mountain and exploded. So many of them went off at once that the entire mountain looked like it was on fire. It became a volcano with plumes and geysers of earth.

Shock waves blasted Ethan's wasp even though it was a mile away in the air.

He felt like he was dying.

Dr. Irving was in there. All of the adult Resisters. Even little kids not old enough to fly sorties.

And they were all getting killed.

Some dust cleared, revealing angled steel struts, the outer layers of the underground base. The Ch'zar were breaking through.

How long until the enemy's mind control got to the colonel and the others?

The next Ch'zar command carrier moved over the mountain and dropped its bombs.

"Stop it!" Ethan screamed.

The detonations heated steel walls, leaving pockmarks and molten craters and gaping holes.

"This is Colonel Winter." A ragged voice came over an open radio channel. "I am the leader of the Resisters and speak for all free humans. You will *not* take us alive."

"Mom, no!" Felix cried over the radio. "Ethan, quick, we've got to get away!"

Ethan couldn't respond. He couldn't even move.

"Everyone!" Felix shouted over the squadron radio channel. "Follow me. Fast!"

His rhinoceros beetle turned and its jets flared. He crashed into Ethan hovering there. He pulled him along as he accelerated away from the Seed Bank as fast as he could fly.

The other I.C.E.s of Sterling Squadron turned and followed.

The mountain exploded, but not from Ch'zar bombs. It exploded from the *inside*.

For a split second, as the mountain cracked into a million pieces, the brightest light Ethan had ever seen came from inside.

Filters instantly clicked into place over the viewscreen, but his eyes burned with jagged afterimages.

The mountain slopes blew out and up and became a fiery mushroom cloud that enveloped the Ch'zar carriers overhead and obliterated them. Roiling shock waves spread out along the ground, igniting thousands of army ants, centipedes, and ant lions, each flaring like a tiny birthday candle.

Radiation warnings clicked within Ethan's cockpit but quickly died down as he continued to rocket away within Felix's grasp.

Over the radio channel, Ethan heard Felix sobbing, but Ethan couldn't cry. Something inside him had broken and no tears came.

The mountain, the Seed Bank, it was all gone.

What remained was a rising pillar of flame that ignited the air around it, sucked in the surrounding oxygen as it kept getting hotter, and rose and rolled into a ball of pure destruction and unimaginable heat.

Colonel Winter had destroyed the Seed Bank rather than let the enemy take them.

That had been the right decision.

The only decision.

But it also meant she was gone. So were Dr. Irving and all the others.

The Resistance was over.

SECOND CHANCE

ETHAN WASN'T SURE WHERE THEY WERE.

They'd flown south for an hour and landed in a scrub pine forest, in a clearing made by nine I.C.E.s flattening the trees and brush.

Ocean waves crashed beyond nearby sand dunes. That had to be the Gulf of Mexico.

Ethan didn't care, though.

After the self-destruction of the Seed Bank, he'd gone numb and had barely been able to pilot his wasp and follow Felix to this place.

Felix's rhinoceros beetle overturned a huge rock, revealing a concrete bunker underneath the size of a swimming pool. Inside was a juvenile luna moth carrier. Its moon-silver scales were covered in dust. Ethan could barely sense the creature's mind. The insect brain had been in deep hibernation mode for a long time.

The Resisters got out of their cockpits. Ethan fell to his knees on the leaf-covered ground, crawled to a mossy rock, and hunkered on it.

Felix jumped into the bunker and inspected the moth and a few dozen barrels marked HYDRAZINE FUEL, AMMO, MRES, POTABLE WATER, and MED.

Felix had explained Special Order 88 on the flight. Each Resister NCO memorized the location of one hidden supply cache for extended missions—or emergencies like this. Special Order 88 was an instruction to reach the cache and take everything you could grab.

Kind of pointless now.

Ethan felt like his insides had been scooped out with a spoon and now he was only a hollow shell of *Lieutenant* Ethan Blackwood.

For the first time in his life, he didn't know what to do, but he no longer cared. He'd failed the Resistance. Had Ethan found a new base or found some way to control the robots in New Taos, the Resisters might've had some sort of chance.

Now? It was futile.

Felix didn't seem to get it. He kept moving, giving orders, getting the other pilots to set up the biomonitors and rouse the luna moth to a wakeful state. He organized the transfer of supply barrels into the moth and set watch using the radar in their I.C.E.s to track inbound enemies.

All Ethan had the energy to do was watch them, at least watch the Sterling kids work. Sure, they'd been horrified to see the Seed Bank get destroyed, but they didn't have families there. In fact, the Sterling recruits had always been on their own. They seemed to thrive on this new impossible challenge. Even Angel was up and moving, although she still looked a little green. She was chewing bubble gum again.

Paul and Madison, though, sat huddled together. They looked like someone had knocked them on the head. They stared off into the distance with glassy eyes. Everyone they'd known—Madison's grandfather and her parents included—had been killed today.

Ethan couldn't guess what that felt like. He had no idea what to say to them.

And at that moment, he was glad he felt nothing.

Felix checked on Madison and Paul but couldn't get them to stir. He shook his head and then walked over to Ethan.

"I need you to wake the moth," Felix told Ethan. "I

know you can get a quick hot-wire mental link. I've seen you do it with your wasp. Otherwise it'll take eight hours to run the start-up protocol. We don't have that much time."

"Try Emma."

"I did. She can't," Felix told him.

Ethan stared at his friend. Felix's face was covered with soot and stained from crying. Somehow, though, he looked stronger and more determined than Ethan had ever seen him.

Didn't Felix realize that they'd all *lost*?

"How can you just sit there?" Felix whispered, almost pleading with him.

"How can *you* keep going, Felix? After everyone—"

Sudden anger flashed over Felix's features, and Ethan shut up.

Felix sighed and his chin quivered. "Don't," Felix said, and stepped back. "If you can help me, then do it. Otherwise don't talk about *them*." He turned his back on Ethan. "I can't talk about her. If I stop now, I'll fall apart, Ethan. I won't let that happen."

Felix waited for Ethan to respond or get up and help.

Ethan had nothing to give his friend.

Felix marched off. He went to Emma, who was trying

to get the diagnostic computer hooked to the luna moth. They spoke, and Emma shook her head in disgust.

Thankfully she didn't come over to chew Ethan out. He couldn't take her hate on top of everything else.

Ethan didn't understand his sister anymore. It wasn't that she was a year older than him. She had more confidence than she'd ever had. New weird mental powers, too.

She and Felix should be leading them.

"I know you'll find a way to make it. The Resistance will live on through you."

Those had been Colonel Winter's last words to him. She'd meant for *him* to lead the others.

That was impossible.

Ethan hugged his knees. He couldn't deal with any of this. Besides the guilt over failing his mission to find a new base for the Resistance and the realization that everyone might be dead because of him, there was the *biggest* failure yet to deal with.

The human race was doomed.

The Ch'zar had won.

Even if Felix could make that food, water, and fuel last a long time, they were all going to grow up. Without an underground refuge to protect them from the Ch'zar mind control, one by one they'd eventually succumb to the aliens.

Or would they?

Emma seemed to be able to hold off the song of the Collective—for now. Could she and Ethan go on? Hide within a neighborhood like their parents had?

A strange mix of homesickness and anger flooded through Ethan. He missed his parents so much. He wished they were here to tell him what to do. He wished they'd told him *something*! He wished they'd given a clue how to survive before they'd abandoned them. Besides that stupid note.

He got up, went to his wasp, and opened the cargo hatch. He rummaged through the gear and took out a crumpled piece of paper.

He read his parents' note for the gazillionth time.

It is our wish one day that we'll all be reunited under the open sky—then we will explain everything.

Like any of that was different from the rest of the lies he'd grown up with.

There was something wrong with his note, though. Or, at least, *his* note was different from *Emma's* note. Just little things, a few words changed, and there was a date on her letter but not on his.

Ethan felt the despair that had been filling him drain away.

Those changes on their notes had even been made on the draft he and Emma had found in their parents' safe in Santa Blanca. They'd gone to *a lot* of trouble to make those changes—right when the mind-controlled adults of Santa Blanca were closing in on them.

Why bother?

Ethan's strength returned and he clenched his fist.

He had an idea why his parents had done it—a crazy, impossible idea but an idea nonetheless, and the only one that made sense: there was a *second* Resistance movement out there, and they'd left him a message.

° ° ° 25 ° ° °

A CODED MESSAGE

ETHAN LAID OUT HIS AND EMMA'S NOTES SIDE BY side on the rock. A tiny beetle crawled over the pages, and Ethan gently brushed it aside.

"I don't see it," Emma told him, refusing to even look.

He'd gotten his sister and her note, and taken her away from the others. He could feel her irritation toward him, bristling like a venomous porcupine.

"Just *look* at them," he told her. "Compare the words."

Emma sighed like this was the biggest imposition in the universe and sat down next to him with a thump, finally glancing sideways at the pages.

First was the note Ethan's parents had left him:

Ethan,

We wish we could explain. If you've come back to save Emma and the twins, though, you must know part of the truth.

And you know why we cannot explain.

We have the twins. We'll be safe.

Emma is likely already at the school. They took her to wait for the zeppelin. There's nothing any of us can do for her now.

The priority is to save yourself. You're more important to humanity than you can know.

Be safe, darling. Keep your head.

It is our wish one day that we'll all be reunited under the open sky—then we will explain everything.

All our love,
Mom and Dad

Then Emma's note:

31st May

Emma,

We wish we could explain. You can't come back to save us, though. You might suspect part of the truth. If you do, you will know why we cannot explain. We will be safe.

Ethan is likely already gone. There's nothing any of us can do for him now.

The priority is to save yourself. You're more important to humanity than you can know.

Be safe, darling. Keep your head.

It is our wish that someday there will be zero trouble and the four of us will be reunited under the open sky; then the two of us will explain everything.

Two big hugs,
Mom and Dad

"You see it?" he asked her.

"Sure, they're different. A little. So what? That doesn't—"

"And remember how there was that draft of the note in their secret safe?"

The annoyance on Emma's face melted away as she remembered.

Ethan went on. "All the differences were crossed out. Mom and Dad were making a—"

"Code," Emma whispered. "One that you could only figure out if you had *both* notes *together*. One that only the two of *us* could figure out if the Ch'zar didn't get us."

She pored over the two letters with new interest, pulled out a notebook from her flight suit, and jotted down a few words.

"There are tons of differences," she said. "I never saw them all before."

"The important words, I think," Ethan said, elbowing her to one side, "are the ones that mean numbers."

She elbowed him back. "I see that."

Emma wrote down "31st May."

"That's *three*, *one*, and *five*," she explained, "since May is the fifth month of the year."

Ethan pointed to the paragraphs in the middle of his letter. "*Twins* there and there," he said. "That could mean 'two.' "

Emma carefully wrote down "2 2" next to her first numbers.

"The last part has a bunch of them," she said, checking and double-checking and then penciling in: "1 0 4 2."

"Oh," Emma said, looking slightly startled, and penciled in one last number. "There's the ending of my letter: 'Two big hugs.' That's another *two*."

She held her notepad for Ethan to see:

3 1 5 2 2 1 0 4 2 2

They stared at the numbers.

They didn't mean anything to Ethan.

"The combination to a safe somewhere?" Emma asked.

Ethan shook his head. "That doesn't feel right . . . like there are too many numbers." He chewed his lower lip, concentrating. "Maybe 'May' in the date isn't supposed to be a number in the code."

"Okay." Emma crossed out the 5, which left:

3 1 2 2 1 0 4 2 2

It still made no sense to Ethan, so he split the number in half (more or less), into the first four (3122) and the last five (10422).

He'd been reading numbers like those for weeks on their flight maps.

The answer must've popped into Emma's head at the same time, too, because together they said, "Longitude and latitude!"

Felix gave up trying to coax the luna moth from its

deep slumber and came over to see what they were doing. He glanced at the numbers and immediately understood as well. "Coordinates to where?" he asked.

"Nowhere yet," Ethan said. He pulled a folded map from his flight suit vest pocket. He tapped the map and interfaced with the flight computer inside his wasp. A globe spun into focus on electronic paper.

"We don't know if those numbers mean anything," Ethan explained. "There are no north–south or east–west designators to go with the latitude and longitude."

"I bet we can eliminate some of the possible combinations," Emma said, tracing her finger over the world. "Thirty-one south latitude, east or west, is in the ocean."

"One-oh-four east longitude is in China," Felix noted, still not understanding but playing along. "Too much radiation there for anything but glowing glass."

"Here," Ethan said, pointing to 31 north latitude and 104 west longitude. "That used to be Texas."

He spread his fingers apart, zooming in on the spot.

More accurate numbers ticked off alongside the map page: 31.22, 104.22.

The map showed a detailed view of a desert that looked like ancient dried skin from the satellite's vantage. There were scattered patches of sagebrush and a dirt road (or it could've been a rabbit track it was so faint).

"Nowhere," Ethan said, feeling a black hole of disappointment fill him.

He'd been *so* sure his parents' notes meant more than just goodbye.

"There has to be something here," Emma said, her forehead wrinkling with confusion and concentration. "That spot just *feels* right."

Ethan felt it, too. There *was* something there. Even if it didn't show up on the map.

Felix's shoulders sagged, and his chest heaved with a shuddering sigh. "I don't know what you're looking for . . . but I'm so tired, guys. And I can't get the stupid moth to wake up. I think it's dead."

That seemed to be the last straw for indestructible Felix. Tears streamed down his cheeks and he hung his head.

Emma gave him a hug. "It's okay," she whispered.

Ethan didn't know how she could say that, all things considered, but he patted Felix on the back to try and make him feel better.

He needed Felix now more than ever.

Ethan glanced at the map to get their current location. They were on the Louisiana coast. All they had to do was dodge a few radiation zones and they could be in West Texas in an hour.

There was one thing, though, that Ethan had to repair before they could even try. It wasn't refueling or getting their I.C.E. weapons recharged and reloaded. While he'd been sitting around feeling sorry for himself, he had forgotten to protect the most important thing in his squadron: his people.

They were broken, exhausted, and demoralized.

He had to lead them. He owed it to everyone in the Seed Bank who'd died protecting them. That was his duty.

Harder than that . . . Ethan had to tell them the truth.

° ° ° 26 ° ° °

SECRET THINGS

ETHAN PLUCKED UP THE TWO NOTES. HE CALLED out to his team, "Stop whatever you're working on. We have a new plan."

The Sterling kids climbed out of the hidden bunker. Madison and Paul, though, sat where they were. So Ethan took a few steps closer so they could hear, too.

"I have a few things to tell you guys. Secret things. But there's no reason for secrets anymore."

Emma whispered, "*What* are you doing?"

He looked his sister in the eye and didn't back down. This was the right thing to do and she knew it.

Emma blinked, pursed her lips, and nodded.

"Emma and I came from a neighborhood," Ethan told them. "We were always different, though."

Angel's gaze focused to laser intensity when Ethan mentioned being different. She winked at him.

Ethan felt uncomfortable whenever Angel looked at him that way, as if he needed more reasons to feel uncomfortable right now.

"Our parents were different, too," Ethan said. "They taught Emma and me to think for ourselves. And when I discovered what the world was really like, they didn't try and capture me; they tried to *warn* me about the Ch'zar."

At this, Paul, Madison, and Felix traded confused looks. Ethan had never told them this part of his story. He was worried about what the Resisters would think of him.

"It had to be a Ch'zar trick," Paul muttered. "Every single adult in those neighborhoods belongs to the Collective. They can't help it. People get older, go through puberty, and their brains get taken over."

"That's what Ethan is trying to tell you," Emma said. "*Our parents* weren't. They learned how to shield their brains."

"That's impossible," Madison whispered.

"It's not," Emma told her. "I've done it. You saw it,

Madison, when we faced down that ant lion in Santa Blanca."

Madison went pale. "And you waited until *now* to tell us this?" Her voice broke with anger. "Don't you think the Resistance could've used that information a while ago?"

"It wasn't until we went back to our neighborhood that we figured most of this out," Ethan told her.

Madison had suspected part of this. So had Ethan. He just hadn't put all the pieces together until he'd seen those two notes side by side.

Oliver held up his hand. He pushed up his glasses. "It's all fascinating, Ethan, but what does that have to do with us now?"

"Our parents left us a clue," Ethan told him. "Coordinates to something. They made it so Emma and I had to be together to find it. But I don't think they could've cooked it up by themselves—two people coincidentally immune to Ch'zar mind control in Santa Blanca. I think they belong to *another* resistance."

Everyone stared at Ethan for a long moment.

"No offense, Ethan," Felix finally said, "but we would've known about another organization fighting the aliens."

"Would you?" Emma asked, and crossed her arms. "If they were silently immune to the Collective's influence and blending in among hundreds of others? It's not like everyone in the neighborhoods wears T-shirts that say 'mind controlled.'"

Paul stood and brushed off his flight suit. "Count me out of this craziness, Blackwoods." He started plodding toward the distant sand dunes. "I'll try and figure out how to make it on my own."

"You can't, Paul," Ethan said, his tone frosty.

"Save it," Paul snapped. "You're not giving orders anymore. There're no more ranks. No more Resistance. Just us survivors."

"You won't last long," Kristov said, trying to sound sympathetic.

Paul shrugged. "Maybe. Maybe not."

"I'm not *ordering* you," Ethan said, and took a step closer. "I'm *telling* you. I need every pilot and every I.C.E. if we're going to survive without the Seed Bank. There's no choice."

The tension in the air seemed to pull taut between the two boys as they glared at one another.

Ethan couldn't afford a mutiny now. If he had to knock Paul's lights out and stuff him into his mantis, locking the controls on autopilot, he'd do it.

Paul balled his hands into fists.

Ethan made fists, too.

This was going to get ugly.

Angel jumped between the boys. "I *like* this plan." She shot a sideways glance at Paul along with a wry smile. "Besides, I'm from Texas. It'll be like going home."

Paul considered Angel for a long time; then he finally shook his head and smiled. "Why not? I'll tag along and keep Angel company. Maybe there is a second Resister outpost in the middle of the desert. Maybe we'll find a herd of purple unicorns, too."

Ethan ignored the sarcasm. He knew it was the best he could expect from Paul Hicks under the circumstances.

"Do we leave the moth and supplies?" Felix asked, unsure. "We'll need them."

"The moth comes with us," Ethan told his friend. Feeling energized, he marched to the edge of the emergency supply bunker.

Ethan held up his hands, closed his eyes, and imagined touching the truck-sized moth. His mind found the insect brain: a small spark in the darkness. Ethan breathed on it like he'd puff on a fire to get it going. Sparks flared, and thought pathways and preflight subroutines booted.

The long-slumbering creature *wanted* to fly. It longed to see the moon again.

Ethan opened his eyes and gestured for the giant insect to rise. Its jets sputtered and coughed soot. Exhaust ducts angled down and roared with fire, making the moth hover out from the bunker. It sat on the ground with a tremendous thud and a flutter of scaled wings.

"Luna moth combat carrier, serial number eight-five-nine-JK, code-named Io, ready for duty," Ethan told Felix.

Felix's mouth dropped open. He closed it with a clack of his teeth and nodded his approval.

"So let's move out," Ethan told everyone.

The members of Sterling Squadron climbed into their I.C.E.s . . . except Madison. She remained sitting on the ground.

"I can't do this," she whispered. "I want to help, Ethan, but there's nothing left inside me." She rested her head on her knees and started to cry.

Ethan took her hand and gave her a gentle pull.

"I need you," he said. "I can't make this work without you, Madison. You've been with me from the start. You have to be with me when it ends."

She looked up, tears glistening in her eyes, her pixie face contorted with grief.

But she nodded and let Ethan help her to her feet.

Wordlessly she hugged him. He hugged her back, and then she gently pushed him away and trod to her waiting dragonfly.

Ethan stared after her, and then at the note and map he held.

There had better be something out there in the middle of nowhere. . . . His people couldn't take another disappointment. Otherwise, this would be the last flight of the last of Sterling Squadron.

○ ○ ○ 27 ○ ○ ○

MIDDLE OF NOWHERE

FIVE HUNDRED MILES AND NO SIGHT OF ANY Ch'zar in pursuit.

Ethan didn't trust that. He'd have thought there'd be patrols looking for the last surviving Resisters.

Of course, the Ch'zar had lost three command carriers, dozens of squadrons, and thousands of ground I.C.E.s when Colonel Winter had detonated a nuclear device inside the mountain.

Ethan curled inward, trying to cradle his aching stomach in the confined space of the wasp's cockpit. He still felt like he'd been kicked in the gut. He couldn't stop replaying the vision of the Seed Bank erupting like a volcano.

A proximity warning chimed. He had drifted within thirty feet of Kristov's locust.

Ethan blinked, course-corrected, and refocused. There was no room for bone-numbing grief when piloting a three-ton insect at five hundred miles an hour. He pushed his thoughts of Colonel Winter, Dr. Irving, and all the others aside. He still had his squadron, and right now they needed him.

Ethan brought up the satellite image of West Texas.

Dry riverbeds snaked through an arid desert. Tiny oases dotted the southern part of the area, but Ethan detected radiation hot spots there, which looked like lime-green measles on his map.

He also spotted fifty-foot-high towers, but when he zoomed in on the image, Ethan found they were nothing but columns of eroded dirt.

"What are those?" Ethan asked on the squadron's radio channel.

"Termite towers," Felix said.

"There are Ch'zar out here?"

"Not exactly," Felix replied. "We've seen colony chimneys before in the deep desert. There are never any termites, though, even when we blast deep. I think they were part of a failed Ch'zar experiment."

Ethan switched to the infrared spectrum and saw no

thermal variations in the terrain under the towers. Empty, like Felix said. Still . . . he couldn't stop thinking of the possibility of a million mutated termites seething underground. Gross.

He gazed west. The sun was low in the sky. That's where they needed to go.

Ethan couldn't say why he felt like he had to get there. Maybe it was some mental link to whatever was at those coordinates. Maybe it was wishful (and foolish) thinking. Or maybe the things shaping his brain were also driving him nuts.

"Disengage weapon safeties," he told the squadron. "I don't want to get surprised up here."

Felix opened a private radio channel. "Am I missing something?" he asked Ethan. "I don't see anything."

"We might *not* see anything," Ethan replied on the secure frequency. "Remember when we approached the Seed Bank? The Ch'zar had some way to jam our signals. I don't trust their satellite feeds either."

"Roger that," Felix said. "My weapons are hot."

Ethan flipped off his stinger laser interlocks and started the warm-up cycle.

They had to be ready for anything. A Ch'zar ambush. A secret city filled with hostile robots. Missiles dropping out of the streaks of cirrus clouds overhead. Anything.

They were just a few moments away from the designated coordinates.

Still nothing on the satellite network or his external cameras other than dry riverbeds that merged into a huge white alkaline plain.

His navigation system pinged. They were directly over the spot.

"Real nice," Paul said. "Is that a flock of wild geese I see down there?"

"Cut the radio chatter," Ethan snapped.

But Paul was right: this was turning into a wild-goose chase.

What had Ethan done wrong?

"There's nothing on the satellite image," Madison told Ethan.

"I can see—"

"Sorry, Lieutenant," she said. "I mean, there's *nothing* down there. I'm not even seeing the dry lakebed. The satellite feed shows only dunes and a few cactuses."

On Ethan's starboard cockpit display, Madison arranged side-by-side images: one from the satellite feed, the other from her camera that gave a real-time view from thirty-five thousand feet.

Ethan should have been seeing the same patch of desert.

He wasn't.

The dry lakebed was missing from the satellite image. Why would the Ch'zar send a false image through their satellite network?

Or maybe it wasn't them generating the fake image.

Maybe it was someone *else* hiding such an obvious feature from them.

"Squadron, go winged flight," Ethan ordered.

His jets cut out and the wasp's wings buzzed. The I.C.E.s slowed and filled the air with blurred wings as they circled back to the lakebed for another look.

"Okay," Ethan murmured to himself. "What's so special it needs hiding?"

"We're landing," he told the others.

The squadron fluttered to the desert floor, kicking up dust and salt as the I.C.E.s landed.

Ethan powered down but left the wasp's laser in preheat mode. This still didn't feel right.

He jumped out of the cockpit and his boots crunched over dried mud scales. This place hadn't seen water in decades. He tasted salt on his lips and smelled an alkaline battery scent in the air.

There wasn't a single footprint or tire tread as far as he could see.

His squadmates gathered around him.

Paul looked smug and his smile drew the scars on his face tight. It was a *told you so, stupid* smile.

Ethan wanted to wipe that smile off Paul's face with his fist, once and for all.

Emma glanced around, transfixed for a moment, and then said, "Come on, it's this way."

"*What's* that way?" Paul asked, looking at her like she was crazy. "There's nothing here!"

Ethan, Madison, and Felix followed Emma as she jogged across the dry lake.

The Sterling kids seemed uncertain what was going on—or who to follow.

Ethan felt it now, too. That magnetic attraction he'd experienced in the air, only ten times stronger down here. Whatever the truth was, Emma was on to *something*.

He ran to catch up with her.

"Hey!" Paul called after them. "What the heck are you running to?" He threw up his hands in disgust.

Kristov and Angel started after Ethan and the others, and then so did Oliver and Lee.

Paul, left standing by himself, finally let out an exasperated growl and trotted after the rest of the squadron.

Ethan jogged alongside Emma. With every stride, he became more sure that what he was searching for was here.

There *was* something out there. A line. No, a shadow. Something or someone stood in the middle of the dry lakebed.

Ethan sprinted ahead. Emma caught up like this was a race.

He got a crazy idea that it had to be his mom or dad . . . waiting for them.

The outline wavered, became bumpy and lumpy, and turned out to be a stack of stones only four feet tall.

The sensation in Ethan's head got stronger with every step toward those stones. It made no sense.

"Just a pile of rocks," he whispered. "All this has been for nothing."

"A pile of rocks *stacked* here," Emma corrected. "Someone had to do that."

That was true. Nowhere else on the lakebed were there stones like this.

"Another clue?" Ethan asked. He gazed at his sister, who nodded, and together they knocked over the stones, moving rocks, looking for whatever was drawing them to the spot.

The last rock sat atop a rusty metal plate. On the surface of this plate were the words TITAN POWER DISTRICT— METER 09112.

"An electrical meter?" Emma said, utterly disappointed.

"This place might've once been a neighborhood," Ethan offered.

He refused to believe it was just an ancient power meter. He pulled off the cover and inside found a single electric switch. It was the kind with a double contact, like you'd see in some old Frankenstein movie.

He closed the circuit. It sparked to life.

Paul and the others finally caught up. "What'd you find?" he said, panting, crowding closer.

"Some switch," Ethan explained, and pointed halfheartedly at the box in the ground.

"There's nothing out here to power up," Oliver said.

Ethan trembled. He wasn't sure if it was anger at Paul, or at himself because this was all for nothing, or maybe he shook because he was still trying to cope with losing the Seed Bank and everyone in the Resistance.

His head felt like it was splitting apart, too.

Dust rose from the dry lakebed.

A crack appeared ten paces from where they stood. Air sucked into the space.

The split elongated, unzipped along the desert floor as quickly as Ethan could follow it—a hundred feet long and then two hundred feet across.

The crack pulled farther apart, yawning like some giant mouth, sand spilling into the darkness beyond.

The feeling that had been building inside Ethan's head up to this point seemed to click in place and stop.

As the gap widened, titanium plates dilated open, and as the fading sunlight penetrated deeper, he saw a man-made tunnel, bristling with missiles and anti-aircraft gun turrets that spun to life . . . and aimed at them.

° ° ° **28** ° ° °

TITAN BASE

ETHAN AND EMMA HUDDLED AROUND THEIR lantern and watched the power panel. LED indicators pulsed with barely visible flickers.

They were inside the control room of the base. Madison had already dubbed it Titan Base, after the Titan Power Company, whose switch had opened the main flight-bay hatch.

It'd taken all night to find the power core and this auxiliary control room.

There was no time for sleep, though. They needed that power now.

Opening the flight-bay hatch had drained almost all

the energy from the base's reserve batteries. They were down to the last 2 percent. If they didn't get the hole in the dry lakebed sealed, the Ch'zar would spot it sooner or later. Sooner, probably.

Ethan had sent the Sterling kids to see if there was a way to crank the massive doors shut manually. No luck so far. Although Oliver was trying to use their I.C.E.s to pull them closed.

"Felix, Madison, Paul, come in," Ethan said into the radio.

Static filled the speakers of the control room.

"Be patient," Emma warned him. "The batteries won't last if you keep asking for reports every fifteen seconds."

Ethan exhaled his frustration.

He had let the others prime the fusion reactor they'd found on the thirtieth sublevel of the base. There was nothing wrong with the reactor. Madison had said it was in perfect working order. It just had to be turned on.

Of course, rebooting a machine that needed a million-degree spark to fuse hydrogen into helium wasn't so simple.

And while the three Resister pilots had basic training in operating the Seed Bank's fusion generators, that was all theory. None of them had actually ever worked on one. If they got it wrong now, they could blow up the reactor, the base, and themselves.

"Almost ready for a prefire test," Madison's voice crackled over the radio. "If that works, Felix is going to manually open the fuel tanks and go for a sustained reaction in the main chamber."

Paul chimed in, "And if that doesn't work, I got two sticks I can rub together down here, Lieutenant."

Ethan let that last comment go. He wasn't sure if one day he'd snap and punch Paul, or if he was almost coming to appreciate his razor-sharp sarcasm.

"What do you need us to do?" Ethan asked.

Felix answered this time. "Get ready to divert the last reserve battery power down to the capacitors," he said.

"Roger that," Ethan replied. "Stand by. . . ."

Emma and Ethan flipped switches and managed to coax the wavering computer display to show the energy pathways needed to charge the reactor's capacitors.

"That's going to be the last of our battery power," Emma whispered. "We won't get a second chance at this."

Ethan nodded. "We're ready up here, Felix. On your mark."

"Okay," Felix replied. "A few more tests. Hang on a second."

Ethan and Emma waited and fidgeted in the gloom. The lights on the control panel flickered. Their lantern started to dim.

Ethan drummed his fingers. It was driving him crazy just sitting here.

Meanwhile, Emma took out the photograph they'd found in the control room. The thing had been there waiting for them. If Ethan hadn't known better, he'd have said *it* was the thing psychically calling him and Emma to this spot.

She placed the yellowed photograph of their parents on the computer display. It backlit the picture, making it easier for them to see their parents' faces.

Ethan's heart fluttered every time he looked at it.

This one old photograph was the emotional equivalent of an overloading fusion reactor.

In the photo, his mom and dad looked fifteen years younger. Together they held a baby swaddled in a pink blanket. They looked down on her with expressions of pure love.

Ethan assumed the baby was Emma. He was born a year later in Santa Blanca General Hospital.

Melinda and Franklin Blackwood wore white uniforms in the picture. There was no special military insignia except for a silver sideways infinity symbol on their lapels.

They sat in this very control room, although back then, every light and indicator was on.

The expression on their faces, though, was totally

different from any Ethan had ever seen on his parents. Along with the adoration for baby Emma, there was worry in their eyes, almost verging on fear. It was as if they knew shortly they'd have to be in a neighborhood surrounded by mind-controlled slaves, in the greatest danger of their lives. They'd be bringing their new daughter as well.

Why would any parent do such a thing?

Ethan touched the picture. Under his fingertips the paper was slick.

It felt real, but it was so unreal, too.

Sure, it confirmed some theories about his mom and dad. They'd been part of something else—call it another resistance against the Ch'zar. They'd been free-willed and living outside Santa Blanca before moving into the neighborhood. They had set up that secret code in his and Emma's goodbye notes because they wanted them to find this place.

There was more, though.

He flipped the picture over.

Written on the back in his mom's neat cursive script was:

Project Prometheus—Phase 4

Ethan grabbed his backpack and pulled out the data crystal he'd gotten (and almost forgotten about) from the library in New Taos. It gleamed like a ruby in the dim light of the control room.

"Prometheus" is what the librarian had called a project that involved "mind expansion," "extrasensory perception," and "group-thought protocols." It'd started before the end of the world war and apparently was still going on until a few years ago with something called Phase 4.

What did it have to do with his parents? What did it have to do with Emma and him?

Ethan turned the crystal over in his hand. If they got the power up and running, he might be able to find a reader to extract more answers from this thing.

But did he *want* to know more?

Did he really want to know what kind of parents would take their kids into a neighborhood, knowing the Ch'zar would come to collect them one day?

"We're ready for you to divert power to the capacitors," Felix said over the radio. "At full charge, we'll fire up the reactor."

"Understood," Ethan replied.

Yeah, they'd fire up the reactor and it'd have a stable

burn . . . or it'd sputter out and leave them in a dead base . . . or the reactor would blow up and send them all to the moon.

He nodded at Emma.

She flipped the manual override switch and diverted the last energy from their reserves.

Ethan crossed his fingers.

"Capacitors at full charge," Felix announced. "Prefire test in three . . . two . . . one . . ."

The lights in the control room went dark, then flared to life and wavered.

"Fusion ignition successful," Felix said, uncertainty thick in his voice. "But the magnetic fields aren't stabilizing."

Computer displays in the control room went on, filled with static, and went dark.

"We got it!" Felix cried over the radio. "Fields are stable and symmetric. We're in business."

All lights and displays came on at full brightness. Computers showed a cutaway view of the fusion reactor churning away with a mixture of hydrogen and helium boiling at a billion degrees kelvin. The displays also showed weapon systems active and tracking the airspace over Texas. They showed computer subroutines feeding false visuals into the Ch'zar satellite network.

"Hey!" Oliver called over the radio. "The lakebed doors are shutting! Move those I.C.E.s inside—fast."

"All clear," Kristov reported, sounding slightly panicked. "Landing now."

"Home sweet home," Angel said with a laugh and a smack of her bubble gum.

Ethan and Emma sighed.

"We did it," his sister said. She slumped in her seat. "We're safe. I could use about three days of solid sleep. But I guess we have to explore this place and find out what we can first."

"Yeah," Ethan said. He stared into the depths of the red data crystal. "And no."

Ethan had an uneasy feeling, like he was missing something dreadfully important.

This wouldn't be over until the humans had won and the Ch'zar were gone. Until then, there could be no rest for him.

Ethan keyed the radio. "Listen up, people," he said. "I want our I.C.E.s refueled, recharged, and flight-checked in one hour. We're moving out."

He paused, realizing that he sounded exactly like Colonel Winter using her "follow orders, no nonsense or there'll be a court-martial" tone of voice.

To stop any protests, Ethan added, "People's lives are at stake, so no grumbling."

Felix said, "Consider it done, Lieutenant."

"Why?" Emma asked. She closed her eyes and rubbed her temples.

At that moment, Ethan had never seen his sister so tired. "Before we left the Seed Bank," Ethan whispered, "I told Colonel Winter I wasn't comfortable being in command. She said that's exactly *why* she put me in command."

Emma opened her eyes and shook her head, not understanding.

"I didn't get it either, until just now," Ethan said. "It means that because I'm not comfortable leading, I'm never going to stop trying to be a better leader . . . and I'm never forgetting about anyone I left behind."

Emma's eyes widened. She now understood what they'd forgotten.

There was one more thing. Ethan wouldn't admit this part, but it had to do with Colonel Winter's last words to him: the Resistance would live on through *him*—specifically him, Ethan Blackwood.

Because he was in charge now.

Ethan stood. He held out his hand to his sister.

"Come on," he whispered to Emma. "There's one more fight."

ALWAYS ONE MORE FIGHT

IT WAS ELEVEN O'CLOCK AT NIGHT IN SANTA Blanca. All the kids should have had their homework done hours ago, been tucked into their beds, and been fast asleep. They absolutely, 100 percent should not have been running through the streets and fighting for their lives.

That was, however, exactly what Bobby Buckman was doing. He ducked as a gas grenade arced over his head.

It landed thirty feet away, downwind, and spun on the asphalt, harmless—unless they had to make a break that way, in which case they'd get gassed and pass out.

The adults from the Neighborhood Watch were taking

blind shots at them, still only guessing where they were hiding.

He and two of his Grizzlies teammates, Sara and Leo, had taken refuge behind the Blanca Dairy milk truck that someone had abandoned in the supermarket parking lot.

The adults had chased them here, and Bobby had been forced to abandon the school bus he'd liberated. He told the kids inside to scatter into the neighborhood, watch, wait, and see if his team could lure the adults away . . . but then what?

Bobby hadn't thought through his plan far enough.

What were they going to do if they got away? Run up into the mountains? How much time would that buy them?

It was no use thinking about that. Bobby and his friends had to survive the next five minutes for any of it to matter.

He steeled himself and peeked around the bumper of the truck.

Three adults moved along the edge of the parking lot, searching one by one the cars left from before a town-wide, twenty-four-hour lockdown had been set.

There was no way they'd be getting out that direction.

Once one adult spotted you, they *all* swooped in on the same location at the same time and grabbed you.

He took a deep breath and forced down the panic rising inside him.

Maybe they could hide inside the milk truck, lock the doors, and hope no one could see in back.

Bobby snuck to the rear door. It was open.

He eased inside, crawled to the front, and motioned for Leo and Sara to follow him. By some freakish good luck, the keys were in the ignition.

Bobby decided to make a break for it. They were sitting ducks here otherwise.

He'd seen his mom and dad drive the family minivan for years. He should be able to work one stupid truck.

At the thought of his mom and dad, though, a lump formed in his throat.

Four days ago, they'd told him that he was sick, that he needed to take one of those new buses to the hospital facility in Terra Nova, West Virginia.

Bobby knew something was wrong with them, because he wasn't sick. He also knew something was wrong because none of the "sick" kids had ever come back.

He wished he had been sick.

He wished this had all been some massive, fever-induced hallucination.

He wished he'd never crossed paths with Ethan and Emma Blackwood and learned the truth.

Bobby turned the key in the ignition. The milk truck coughed once, lurched forward, and the engine died.

He cursed, put the truck in park, and tried again.

But the adults had seen.

They moved together toward the truck. It was weird the way they walked, with military precision, like robots inside of humans. It gave Bobby gooseflesh.

He found the courage to turn the ignition again, gave the truck some gas, and the thing roared to life.

Bobby shifted into drive and peeled out, fishtailing through the parking lot, dodging parked cars and light poles.

The driveway to the road was just fifty feet—and then escape.

Bobby floored it, and the truck jumped forward.

The steering wheel spun in his hands, though, no matter how hard he gripped it.

He realized it wasn't only the wheel—the truck slid back and forth, as did the other cars in the parking lot. Even the ground buckled and rippled.

Cracks opened in the asphalt as an ant the size of an eighteen-wheeler stepped from the shadows into the milk truck's path. With each step, the ant's tremendous weight shook the entire parking lot.

Bobby swerved.

The milk truck screeched sideways, tilted, and started to tip.

The ant caught the truck in its steel-crushing jaws.

Behind Bobby, Sara and Leo screamed as the insect lifted the truck off the ground . . . and then it stared into the truck with a ten-foot-wide compound eye.

Bobby would've screamed, too, but he was too terrified. His lungs seemed to have stopped working.

He saw himself reflected a hundred times in the ant's hexagonal eye segments.

This was it. He was going to die, frozen with terror, unable to even try to fight.

And *that* got him mad—enough to snap out of the fear that gripped him.

"Go ahead!" he yelled at the ant. "Try and eat me. I hope you choke!"

The ant hesitated and cocked its head.

Bobby couldn't believe it. Had he actually scared the thing?

The ant dropped the truck.

There was a split second of free fall, and then Bobby and the others slammed onto the metal floor of the truck.

Bobby got to his feet and wobbled. The world spun.

He then saw what had really stopped the ant.

Another giant bug dropped from the sky. An impossibly large blue beetle landed directly on top of the ant.

The beetle's impact crunched chitin as it blasted the ant with a beam weapon projected from the rhinoceros-like horns on its head.

The ant screamed and melted from the intense heat. Boiling gray ichor gushed out from its broken body.

More ants scrambled over and *through* houses to engage this new threat.

A red locust landed and wrestled with one. A dragonfly buzzed over the ground, strafing ants with rapid-fire laser pulses that left Bobby blinking back tears.

A huge ladybug landed with a thud next to the milk truck, and then let loose with a salvo of rocket-propelled bombs that turned the advancing column of ants into pieces of twitching limbs and smoldering shells.

Bobby, ears ringing from the explosions, wondered if he'd been knocked out and this was all some weird dream.

A black-and-gold wasp streaked through the sky, laser flashing. It grabbed the last ant and tossed it aside, leveling the corner newsstand in the process.

This was no dream.

Bobby had seen these giant bugs before.

"Blackwood," he muttered.

Bobby clambered toward the back of the milk truck,

not sure if he was going to kill Ethan Blackwood for leaving him or shake his hand for coming back.

Maybe both.

The wasp landed near the milk truck and its cockpit opened.

The adults at the edge of the parking lot stared at the wasp and at the figure that emerged from it . . . and then they ran.

"I came back," Ethan told Bobby and the other kids. "Like I promised. No one gets left behind anymore."

Ethan looked different from when Bobby had seen him last. Something had happened to him. Something terrible had been etched into his features. There was a new resilience, though, a strength that Bobby had never seen in a classmate—or in any adult, for that matter. There was no fear or doubt left in Ethan Blackwood.

Ethan looked out at the darkness of Santa Blanca and then addressed the adults and the insects he seemed to know were watching and listening: "You think the Resistance is dead. Think again. We're just getting started."

He reached out to Bobby. "We're the Resisters," Ethan told him. "Join us if you want to fight for yourself, for humanity, and for a free Earth."

DON'T MISS THE NEXT BOOK IN
THE RESISTERS SERIES!

COMING IN OCTOBER 2013!

○ ○ ○ ABOUT THE AUTHOR ○ ○ ○

ERIC NYLUND is a *New York Times* bestselling and World Fantasy Award–nominated author. He is also director of narrative design for Microsoft Studios, where he helps create blockbuster video games.

Eric has bachelor's and master's degrees in chemistry. He graduated from the prestigious Clarion West Writers Workshop in 1994. He lives in the Pacific Northwest with his family. You can learn more about Eric and contact him at ericnylund.net.